Also by Eve West Bessier

New Rain: A Visionary Novel
Roots Music: Listening to Jazz
Exposures: Tripod Poems
In the Flow of Grace

Pink Cadillacs

Eve West Bessier

FALCON WEST BOOKS

For Elisabeth and Patrick
with all my love

Acknowledgments

The author wishes to thank the editors of the publications in which the following stories included in this collection first appeared.

"A Ride to the Airport," *The Los Angeles Review*, September 3, 2021.

"Fragile," *Apple in the Dark*, Summer, 2021.

"The Love Tattoo,*" Kalliope, A Journal of Women's Literature and Art*, Vol. 3, No. 1, 2002.

"The World's Largest Ball of Bras," *The Sacramento News & Review*, August 30, 2001.

The following stories in this collection received awards.

"The World's Largest Ball of Bras," *Sacramento News & Review Short Story Contest, Second Place Winner,* 2001.

"The Love Tattoo," First Place Award in the *California Focus on Writers Competition,* 2000.

"The Love Tattoo," solo recipient of the *Kathryn Hohlwein Literary Award,* 2000.

Table of Contents

From the Southwest

From the West Coast

From the South and Further South

Pink Cadillac

(listening to "Take Five" by Dave Brubeck)

I am a 1959 icon, pink as the innocence
of a nation with a yet untainted reputation.
I represent overabundant prosperity, a no-hard-luck
charm, and the charisma that a few bucks can solve
any problem. I am absolved of responsibility,
even Elvis owned a hardtop model of me,
without worry about disowning his masculinity.
Clint Eastwood starred in a film named after me,
and a Grand Marnier cocktail hails my moniker
like a flaming flag in the face of the mundane.
Aretha, singing from my topless beauty on a pink
and white interior was clearly a superior being.
I even drag-queened across the Bible Belt,
like a bottle-blonde Marilyn, with dirt devil
wind blowing across my chrome-edged fins.

From *Roots Music: Listening to Jazz*
by Eve West Bessier

From the Southwest

Breakfast at Maggie's

Sheriff Jack Spencer peeled the foil top off the single serving of creamer. He stared at his cup. It was too full. He leaned down and sipped a bit off the top. It was far from hot. He emptied the creamer carefully. The coffee still sloshed over the rim and spilled onto the saucer. He lifted the cup slowly and sipped. Now it was close to cold and dripped from the bottom of the cup onto the paper placemat, where he'd written a few notes for Dobson.

"Damn," Jack whispered, watching the ink lift and blur. Dobson hadn't shown, so it didn't matter. Scott Dobson was a terrific deputy. He and Jack always met at Maggie's for breakfast before starting their day. Jack had called Dobson twice but only got the dispatcher. Maybe last night's storm had made the roads more impassable than usual. He'd wait another ten minutes, then he'd have to leave.

He had a meeting at the Gallup County Seat. After that, he'd pick up a load of firewood for his uncle. The old ranch house near Twin Lakes was getting more drafty every year. Next weekend he'd go out there and do some repairs. For now, he'd make sure the old man had enough wood to stave off the chill. He wasn't sure how long Uncle Joe could continue to live alone, but the man was a stubborn goat and not likely to leave until, as Joe himself put it, he was taken out feet first in a cedar box.

Jack stared out the window. There was a semi parked by the gas station. Maggie's Ranchero and Fred's Chevy truck were near the kitchen. He'd borrowed his girlfriend's old Ford Ranger again for a couple of days. She was getting tired of his car problems. So was he. The department Jeep was getting another patch job at the shop. For a moment he caught his own reflection in the glass. His hair was graying at the temples, but on top it was still solid black. He should grow a mustache. He thought his upper lip looked kind of weak. It struck him that he was looking more and more like his father. He frowned.

He shifted his focus back to the parking lot. There were only two cars he didn't recognize: a blue Honda Civic and a white Dodge commercial van with Gomez Heating and Air painted on the side. Not a local company as far as he knew, must be passing through. The Civic probably belonged to the new waitress. Where was she? He really wanted some hot coffee. He hadn't slept well last night with the storm banging all the loose ends of his life around.

The wind was still vicious this morning. Maggie's Cadillac Cafe sign, shaped like the classic car's tail fin, oscillated with a high-pitched squeak. The cafe had been a real looker in its Route 66 glory days, but was now sadly in need of repairs that Maggie couldn't afford. Still, it had its charm. The booths were red vinyl and each still had its vintage Select-O-Matic jukebox controller at the back edge of the formica table top. There was no longer an actual jukebox in the diner, so the remote controllers were a moot point, but a nice homage to the past.

Over the years, customers had given Maggie to-scale models of classic Cadillacs. She had glued the toy cars precariously to the tops of the chrome juke controllers. Jack was sitting in the 1955 Eldorado booth. His favorite for the view. The miniature Eldorado convertible was cherry red, but the New Mexico sun had faded the side facing the window to a soft pink. Jack had long been tempted to turn the car around, so it could fade to pink on the other side as well. Make things even, balanced.

Maybe today was the day. He made sure Maggie wasn't looking his way, then tested the Eldorado to see if it was still firmly attached. It wasn't. The Super Glue on the toy's plastic tires had become crispy in the dry desert air. He *could* do it, but he'd be a fool to think Maggie wouldn't notice, and a bigger one to mess with the order of things in her domain. He left the car in its original orientation.

Jack scooted to the edge of the booth, leaned out and looked around. No waitress, but his adrenals gave his heart a quick punch.

How long had *she* been sitting there? The plate of half-eaten flapjacks indicated a while. She was facing almost completely away from him. She was wearing faded jeans, cowboy boots, and a black sweater. She looked small, tired, too skinny.

She must've come in after he was seated in the booth. He was facing away from the door. But how had he missed seeing her walk in from the parking lot? His keen investigative skills were slipping, too much desk work lately. Did she sell her Toyota? Did she go into the heating and air business? That made him smile, just for a moment, as he imagined her inching through the crawlspace under some house to find the faulty duct. She was deathly afraid of spiders and snakes. Bit of a problem for a desert dweller.

She seemed preoccupied, staring at Maggie's bowling trophy display up behind the counter. He knew she had no interest in bowling and wondered what she was thinking.

"Damn," Jack whispered again. Her table was between him and the front door.

Maybe he should go over and talk to her. No. That was a bad idea. The last time he'd done that, they'd had a nasty fight. The looks she'd given him still burned. That had been over four months ago.

She had that job at the Family Dollar in Ya-Ta-Hey, but it couldn't pay much. She could probably use some money. How much cash did he have with him? He'd just spent most of it on gas for the truck. She wouldn't accept it anyway. Too proud. He took a deep breath and let it out slowly.

Maybe she *had* seen him and was choosing to ignore him. She'd gotten good at that. He knew she didn't like his new girlfriend. He was beginning to wonder if he agreed with her on that.

He slumped back into the dip in the center of the vinyl bench and opened the paper's sports section, trying to distract his mind.

After a few minutes, he scooted back to the edge and looked at her again. She hadn't moved. Come on, Hun, he thought, just finish your breakfast and get on with the day. She had always been sort of a dreamer, never in any kind of a hurry. Unlike him.

He looked at his watch. 8:35. He really had to get going.

He didn't mind the dangers of his line of work. Things sometimes got a little rough. People didn't always take kindly to being apprehended. He could handle a physical skirmish. He'd even pull his gun if it was absolutely necessary, but this personal stuff was something else. Women and their entire emotional deal were a minefield, and he had big feet.

Maggie's had a service exit in back, but he'd feel like a complete coward if he used it. Plus, Maggie didn't take kindly to customers traipsing through her kitchen. He'd never hear the end of it.

He downed a couple of sips of the cold coffee just for the caffeine, pulled out his wallet and left enough for the meal and tip under the salt shaker. He left the newspaper for the next customer.

He scooted out of the booth, put on his Carhartt jacket and cowboy hat, then walked as quietly as possible towards the door. Her back was to him now. Her long hair fell in a loose braid, blue-black and shiny as raven feathers.

He turned the doorknob and pulled lightly, the bells still jingled loudly. He glanced back. She didn't turn around to look at him.

"Bye, Pop," she said, just like she used to as a kid. She was always late for the bus, running from the kitchen, lunch pail in hand, hair damp from her bath. Except now, her voice sounded sad.

He stopped breathing for a moment. Was she offering him a chance? A chance for what? He was caught in a tug-of-war with himself, and he didn't have time to talk. Maybe he would call her later. He already knew he probably wouldn't.

"Bye, Rabbit. Gotta go," he explained to the back of her head, wishing he hadn't used her old nickname. She didn't like it anymore. He wished she'd turn around and look at him, but was also sort of grateful that she didn't. "Running late," he added.

"Yeah," she said. Her back, a fortress. "Have a good one."

"You too."

He wanted to say something more. He wanted to tell her again that he'd always love her mother. Sherrie had moved on. It had been two years, he had to move on too. What more could he say? That he was sorry? He wasn't sorry. Not exactly. It was nobody's fault. It was just life. Things changed, but they were her parents and that was forever.

He fully opened the door. The chilled air entered the warmth of the diner. He stepped quickly outside and closed the door behind him.

He stood for a moment in the protected niche created by the diner's two alcoves. He could hear the soft hum of the *Open* sign in the window next to him and the high-pitched whir of a lug nut wrench at the gas station.

He looked down at his feet. A thin layer of red mud caked his boots. They'd be caked with a lot more of it soon. He looked out past the highway towards the mountains. A steel-grey cloud bank approached from the north like a battleship heading in from Canada. The air already smelled like snow. He heard the bells on the door jingle.

She stood next to him.

They both looked at the menacing sky in silence.

"I'm moving," she said.

"Oh, yeah? When?"

She didn't respond for a moment, then said, "Today."

He let that sink in. If he hadn't seen her this morning, would she not have told him?

"Where to?"

"Albuquerque."

"To be with your mom."

"Yeah. She's not doing so great."

"I'm sorry to hear that," he said, and meant it.

He wondered how he had gotten so out of the loop.

"Is there anything I can do?"

"I don't blame you, Pop. I know you think I do."

"You sure seem plenty angry."

"I'm always angry at something, you know that."

"Is your mom gonna be okay?"

"Maybe. Maybe not."

He turned to look at her. This was alarming news.

"I got an appointment," he said, "but it can wait. Wanna go back inside?"

"I need to go, wanna beat this storm."

"I'd like to know how she's doing. I do care."

"I know, Pop."

"You leaving permanently?"

"Not sure."

He knew she'd considered it on and off.

"It's another world down there," he said.

"I've been there lots, Pop."

"Visiting a big city is not the same as calling it home."

"Who says I'm calling it home?"

"You moving your stuff in that Dodge van?"

"Yeah. Cory borrowed it. I'm picking him up after his shift. He's gonna help get my stuff to mom's, then drive back tomorrow."

"You're not taking your Toyota?"

She laughed. "I couldn't even get it started this morning."

"Yeah, it's seen better days."

"Figure I'll use mom's car, 'till I get a job and buy something used."

"Good plan. Promise you'll let me help, okay? You know, money, talk, whatever."

"Sure."

"You want some cash? I haven't got much on me, but it's yours."

"Nah, I'm okay. Thanks."

He turned to face her and reached out his arms, hoping she'd accept a hug.

The force of her coming into his chest surprised him, like she wanted to hide there. He wrapped his arms around her, held her as if she were five years old and afraid of the dark.

Pink Cadillac Ranch

Josh shifted his weight from one cowboy boot to the other on the wooden porch. His two black labs, Wendell and Orville, rested in the shade of the old cottonwood nearby. They looked up once in a while to see if anything was happening. Nothing was.

Josh's ranch sat on the old Turquoise Trail that ran between Albuquerque and Santa Fe. Halfway between the tiny town of Madrid and the ghost town of Cerrillos, the location almost qualified as being in the middle of nowhere. Madrid, pronounced as a combination of the word *mad* and the word *rid*, not like the city in Spain, housed an eccentric collection of old hippies and avant-garde creatives. Cerrillos spoke volumes of history but had only a few living voices. A lonesome ranch between the two might not be the best place for a teen-aged girl, but it would have to do.

Josh could see the dust plume from a car or truck heading up the dirt road in his direction. He waited, keeping his eyes fixed on the tall yellowish swirl, more likely from a truck than a rental car. Then again, Dan might have rented a truck. The plume turned off to the left, it was not them.

His brother texted when he'd arrived at the airport in Albuquerque and should have been here by now. Military dudes follow strict protocol and are never late, but New Mexico could throw a monkey wrench into even the best laid plan.

Josh debated going back inside the cooler house. A watched pot never boils, or so they say, but he felt too antsy.

The lemonade he made this morning was chilled and ready in the fridge to soothe some thirsty travelers. He hadn't seen his niece Andrea, whom everyone called Andie, in five years. Not since Dan transferred to Lewis-McChord Air Force Base south of Seattle. Andie was fifteen now and would be a very different child, a teenager. That made Josh a little nervous as she would be in his care for the next two years while her dad served in Iraq. Andie's mom was currently in rehab for drug and alcohol abuse. Not the first time, and not the best choice of parental guidance until she could clean up and stay clean.

Andie was going to live with her grandparents on the ranch in North Dakota, but Josh's dad had a stroke two months ago. That changed the scenario. Supporting her husband's slow recovery taxed Josh's mom. Having a teen in her care at the same time didn't seem reasonable, so Josh offered to have Andie live with him.

Josh took off his dusty Stetson, the one his dad had sent him a few years back. He wiped his forehead with a red bandana and by the time he looked out towards the road again, there was another dust plume. This time it turned right, towards his ranch. Josh smiled.

He looked down his driveway at the two pink Cadillacs standing sentry on either side of the opened gate. The cars were too debilitated to drive and their original hot pink paint had faded to a dusty rose in the high desert sun. They were a nod to the famous Cadillac Ranch near Amarillo, Texas; though Josh's were not buried hood down with their tail fins up in the air. They faced the driveway, like a couple of aging, ineffective guard dogs just looking for someone to pay them a little attention.

Owning a ranch devoid of cattle and calling it the Pink Cadillac Ranch would be tantamount to asking for big trouble in North Dakota, but here, so close to Madrid and not far from Santa Fe, it was just the right amount of quirky.

Josh didn't exactly consider himself to be an artist, but his kinetic metal sculptures sold well on Canyon Road in Santa Fe. Those sales kept him mostly in the black for five years running now, a respectable stretch. He also boarded horses for wealthy folks who only came out on weekends to ride. He hoped Andie liked horses. That would be a bonus for her, and for him.

A black Ford Explorer turned into the driveway and pulled up next to Josh's red F150.

Josh scooted down the steps to greet them. Dan got out of the SUV and came running up to Josh giving him a bear hug that just about lifted him off the ground. Andie got out and stood next to the car looking awkward and boyish in her faded jeans and black Chuck Taylor high tops. She wore a retro Pink Floyd t-shirt. There might be hope for this uncle-niece relationship.

The Stetson Josh bought for Andie might not be a good fashion fit, just yet. Maybe a little down the road, once living on the ranch and eating tons of green chilies put some southwest into her blood.

Josh gave Andie a goofy smile over her dad's shoulder. She smiled back. They both knew Dan's hugs could last a while and be akin to a chiropractic adjustment.

Once inside, they all sipped lemonade from dark blue Mexican glasses, sitting at the chrome and formica kitchen table, listening to the soft drone of the swamp cooler.

"Hey, you guys hungry?" Josh asked. "I barbecued chicken yesterday. I can make sandwiches."

"We stopped at a Lotta Burger," Dan said. "There was construction near the airport and we weren't moving, so we pulled off for a snack."

That explained why they were later than expected.

"Didn't you get my text?" Dan asked.

"Nope, but this far from a tower, texts often don't come through until they are a moot point," Josh explained.

Just to drive that moot point home, his phone chirped.

"Aha! I'll bet that's your text now," Josh said, checking his phone. "Yup."

"You really are out here in the middle of nowhere!" Dan said.

Andie frowned, just for a moment, but Josh took note. Still, Andie had always been a bit of a loner, so he hoped she'd enjoy it here.

She'd be a lot closer to civilization here than at the family ranch in North Dakota. That fully qualified as the middle of nowhere. Here she'd be about an hour's drive to Albuquerque, forty minutes to the center of Santa Fe. The tiny town of Madrid was just down the road and a real hoot. Josh's friends there were all super excited to welcome Andie. Young pups were not in large supply, except for dogs and coyotes.

"So," Josh said. "Let's get your bags into your room. I hope you'll like it. My friend Ruth insisted on helping pull it together. She might have overdone the southwest theme a bit. She owns an antique store in Madrid and loaned us the furniture plus some decorative things, just to get us started. We can fix the room up just the way you want later, okay?"

"Thanks, Uncle Josh," Andie said.

Josh could guess the state of her heart right now. He and Dan had been shipped off to their aunt's house for a summer when their mom's drinking problem escalated to loud expressions of anger that worried the church ladies enough to intervene. Against the protests of their father, who insisted everything was under control, the boys had been sent away while their mom was given the help she needed to start her arduous journey to sobriety. He'd been fourteen at the time, Dan twelve. Last week, their mom had celebrated twenty years of sobriety.

Josh knew Dan talked with Andie about all of that, but Dan could be emotionally guarded, and maybe Andie could use a less stoic perspective.

Josh wanted to be a supportive uncle without invading Andie's privacy, a tricky balance. Stepping into a father-figure role with no experience to back him up and only a month's notice didn't exactly bolster his confidence.

They took her bags into Andie's new bedroom. She chuckled when she saw it.

Dan actually laughed out loud. "It looks like a Route 66 motel room!" he said. "Fantastic!"

The room expressed western to the max, complete with a bedside lamp that had horses painted on the shade and a plastic cactus as its base. A light blue and beige Navajo style rug hung on the wall above the bed. A multi-colored striped Mexican serape was the bedspread, and there were two Mexican pillows embroidered with bold fuchsia and yellow flowers. Various western curios adorned the bookcase shelves and the old oak dresser. A Mexican chair made of woven wood covered in orange leather sat in the corner by the window.

Angie sat on the bed and ran her hand over the cotton serape.

"This is so cool!"

"Bought that in Mexico myself a few years ago," Josh said.

"It definitely stays!" Andie said. "Actually, I love all of this! Please thank Ruth for me and thank you, Uncle Josh."

A worried look passed over her. "I'm sorry to have to barge in on your life like this."

"Are you kidding?" Josh said. "I'm totally pumped! We haven't had a chance to hang out in so long. We're going to do lots of fun stuff. I'm happy to have you here."

Andie got up and hugged him, just the same way she used to as a little kid, without any awkwardness. That was reassuring.

Josh thought she seemed very together, or at least able to hold it together despite the situation. She'd just left her friends, her comfort zone, her budding teen-aged life behind, and any new life she started here would be interrupted again in just a couple of years. That was par for the course in military families, but it couldn't be easy.

Josh used to spend time with her every week when she was younger and they had all lived in San Diego, but his move to New Mexico and their move to the Northwest made staying in close touch a challenge. It felt great to be a part of her life again.

"You'll be able to thank Ruth yourself," he said. "She's invited us for dinner whenever we're ready to take her up on it. You'll love her. She's a quirky artist in her seventies from Woodstock, New York. No kidding, the real deal. She wears Mexican peasant dresses and still has long, braided hair. A real hippie!"

"Cool."

Josh turned to Dan, "I don't have another bedroom to offer you, Bro. So, I'm afraid it's the couch for you, unless you'd prefer the air mattress?"

"I hate those things," Dan said. "Always feel like I'm about to roll off the edge and I usually do. The couch is perfect."

"I'll keep the dogs in my room at night, so they don't bother you."

"Dang, I was kind of looking forward to the company."

"Well, okay then, you can have Wendell. He's mellow. I'll keep Orville with me, he's a pain in the ass sometimes, especially if he's excited about something new, like house guests."

Dan would be staying for three nights to help Andie get settled in. Then he'd fly back to Seattle before heading out on his Air Force tour of duty.

That was only two full days on the ranch, and they'd make the best of them. Dan hadn't been on a horse in a decade and wanted to ride. He hadn't lost his knack for it. Her father's enthusiasm infected Andie, who gave it a try on a mild, older mare that Josh picked out for her.

She got up into the saddle without any help and didn't show a smidgeon of fear. That was a relief because he really wanted working with the horses to be part of her daily routine. It would be a good distraction and a useful skill, though maybe not so much once she returned to Seattle.

Dan had already enrolled Andie at Capitol High in Santa Fe. The school had students working online from home three days a week and attending in person two days. It was a cost-cutting measure for the school and a helpful thing as the school wasn't close. Josh would take Andie there this year. Next year she'd be able to drive herself. They could start some lessons right away.

He'd thought about fixing up one of the pink Cadillacs for her, but it seemed impractical and not exactly what a teen girl wants to be driving, though what did he know about teen girls? A trustworthy pickup truck made more sense and he didn't want to separate the twin Cadillacs. They'd miss each other's company.

On the morning that Dan had to drive back to Albuquerque, Josh made huevos rancheros with Hatch green chilies, fresh white corn tortillas and refried beans with a dollop of sour cream on top. They also had big mugs of Mexican coffee with vanilla extract.

Josh suggested that he and Andie take a day trip and head out before Dan's departure. That way Andie wouldn't feel left behind. She could do the leaving. A small gesture, but he suspected it might help her to not have to see her dad drive away.

After a long hug and a few tears, Andie climbed into Josh's truck. They waved goodbye to Dan and headed north on the Turquoise Trail. They were going to Bandelier National Monument to check out the Anasazi ruins.

Andie was wearing the new Stetson and loved it. Josh had given it to her now after all. She had on 110 sunblock to protect her sun-deprived skin. They had lots of water with them, plus sandwiches and snacks. Bandalier had shady areas where they could hike under ponderosa pines and aspen to balance out the exposed trails along the ancient cliff dwellings.

Bandalier did not disappoint. Whatever Andie felt inside, she managed to put it aside for the day. They hiked, climbed kiva ladders, ate their sandwiches sitting under the trees, and laughed a lot together over stories from their shared past.

Back at the ranch, they both went to bed early, worn out from the adventure.

Sometime in the night, Josh awoke to the sound of sobbing from the room down the hall. Andie's emotions had caught up with her.

Not surprising, Josh thought, staring at the ceiling. Orville and Wendell stirred and shifted their positions against his feet.

Should he get up and try to comfort her? That's what he wanted to do, his instinctive reaction, but knocking on her door in the middle of the night seemed invasive. She might be embarrassed about her tears.

Josh was stumped, but he couldn't just ignore her pain. He turned on the Himalayan salt lamp by the bed and found his cellphone on the nightstand.

He'd text her. That's how teens communicated. He doubted she turned off her phone, ever. It was her lifeline.

He texted rarely and had no idea how to do it teen style.

"Milk and cookies?" He typed. "Meet you in the kitchen?"

No response for a few moments, but he no longer heard her crying.

"K," she texted back.

Josh got up and went into the kitchen, the dogs followed. The night air came in through the screen door.

Andie arrived with the serape blanket from her bed wrapped around her shoulders, more for emotional than physical comfort, Josh guessed since it was still quite warm in the house.

"I don't think I want any milk or cookies," she said. "Maybe just some cold water."

"You bet," Josh said. "Let's go sit on the porch, cooler out there."

"Sure," she said.

He filled up two trail bottles with chilled water from the fridge, and they headed outside to the wooden porch swing at the edge of the deck where they could see up into the star-filled sky.

The dogs came out and went down the stairs to get the cool dirt of the driveway up against their hot bellies.

Andie looked up into the sky. "Holy crap!"

"I know, amazing, right?"

"I had no idea there were so many of them! You can hardly see any in Seattle, even when it's clear, and it's mostly too cloudy anyway."

"Do you miss home?" Stupid question, Josh thought, kicking himself for asking it.

Andie didn't say anything for a moment.

"Yeah," she finally said. "I do, but also, I don't. At home, I thought about mom all the time. The rehab place is close to the base, so I always felt like I should go there to see her, even when I really didn't have the time, plus they only had certain visiting hours. Here, I can't go see her. That's kind of a relief. Is that sort of mean of me to think that? I do love her."

"I know you do," Josh said.

"Your mom had trouble with alcohol too," Andie said. "I know that from Dad. So, it's okay to talk about stuff like that with me, if you want."

Josh smiled. Here she was, all of fifteen, reassuring him. He knew from experience that having an alcoholic parent forced you to grow up fast, to take on an adult role before you were ready.

"Thanks," Josh said. "Your dad's told you that what's happening with your mom is not in any way your fault, right?"

Andie leaned her head back, studying the stars.

"Yeah, he's said that to me, but I still feel responsible, like having to be my mom was too much for her."

"It sucks," he said. "I really, really get that."

Suddenly, Andie leaned into him on the porch swing. He put his arm around her shoulder.

They sat in silence for a while, staring up at the black bowl of the sky filled with billions of pinprick lights.

"Oh, wow! A shooting star!" Andie said.

"That was a good one too," Josh said. "I come out here a lot. Puts things into perspective."

"I can totally see that. Hey, do you believe in UFOs? I hear that people see them in New Mexico all the time, though Dad says that's a bunch of crap."

"Well, personally, I'm a believer!"

"Cool!"

"So, you really think my mom's drinking is not in any way because of me?"

"It's not, Andie. You are one heck of a great kid, you always have been."

"Thanks, that means a lot."

"You know, adults are responsible for their own behavior. That's part of the definition of being an adult, though sometimes it's not easy. I think your mom would not want you to feel responsible for what's going on with her."

"I'm sorry to be such a downer," Andie said, "and I'm super sorry I woke you up. I had such a scary dream. It totally freaked me out."

"You're not a downer, Andie. I completely understand. Would it help to talk about the dream?"

"No, it wasn't a reality kind of dream. It was one of those weird nightmares that doesn't make any sense. I just have to shake it off. This awesome sky is helping. Thanks."

They sat in silence and sipped some water.

The mountain air from the Sandias dropped down into the valley. Andie wrapped the serape more tightly around her.

"It's getting sort of cold out here," Josh said. "Want to head back inside?"

"Yeah. Okay. I'm getting kind of sleepy too."

"Good, but if you have another scary dream, you can always come knock on my door and wake me up. Anytime you need to not be alone."

"Okay, thanks, Uncle Josh."

"Do you want Wendell to come sleep with you? He's a good old dog and won't keep you awake."

"Sure. I would love that."

"Okay. It's a plan."

"And Uncle Josh,"

"Yes."

"Thanks for saying that, about it not being my fault. It's easier for me to believe it coming from you. When Dad says it, I just figure he has to say it because he's trying to be a good dad, you know."

"Yeah, sure."

They both gazed up into the cosmos one more time.

"Whoa! What was that?" Andie said.

"You mean that super bright light that just went left really, really fast?" Josh said. "Then went straight up really, really fast and disappeared into nowhere?"

"Holy crap! Really?"

"I don't think the military has anything that can do that."

"Cool!"

"You, my dear, have just seen your first UFO!"

"Wait 'till I tell Dad!"

She laughed, "On second thought, he'd just say I'd imagined it."

"You're right, he probably would say that."

"No way did I imagine that!"

"Not unless we both imagined it together at the same exact time!"

"Maybe it can be just our secret, Uncle Josh? I'd like that."

"I'd like that too, very much."

Fragile

The first storm of an early winter descends into the Front Range of the Rockies.

I watch rain pound the canyon.

Late afternoon light slants through the sudden deluge, creating a radiant silver scrim across the pine-green slope of Arkansas Mountain.

It has just turned September, but this rain aspires to hail. It batters against soil, rock, pine and three mountain bikers in high-tech neon on the mud-gray road.

Gravity is an ancient excuse for violent water. The gods are having a fistfight up there; spitting out their icy teeth and their chilled, white blood.

I am dry. I am standing at the edge of changing into someone stronger than I ever wanted to be.

The strength doesn't come willingly. It comes like an angry steer on the end of taught rope. It kicks. It moans. It blows hot breath from its nostrils. Sweat flies off its back and belly. It leaves me spent, vacant.

I am standing in the unfinished sunroom; three walls around me are glass from floor to ceiling. From here, the storm is panoramic. Today, the opened, sliding-glass door leads directly to a thirty-foot drop. The stairs my husband plans to build beyond this threshold are still missing.

I inch out just over the edge, toes testing the precipice. I look down at the slope of rock, mud and juniper. The slight overhang of the roof protects me from the falling torrents of water. Lightning makes me raise my eyes. Thunder follows very close. I shiver. Everything feels immediate, choppy like churned seawater. Risky like living, like dying.

The transient downpour grows dense, obscuring my view. Spruce and pine a hundred feet from the house are sketchy outlines in this wall of milky movement and madness.

If I reach out far enough, the rain's madness will engulf me. If I step out into this clattering curtain, I will fall and break something.

I will connect with stone and no longer be whole. I am already not whole. Perhaps I can break my life into pieces as small and furious as these arrows of rain. Then the wind could wash me down into the canyon's belly where the earth would swallow me.

The earth makes no such promises. I know.

I push up my right sleeve, hold on to the door jamb with my left hand and reach out past the protection of the roof, past the protection of fear, out into the frenzy of weather. My hand and arm soak with the cold of it, the force of it. The rapture of hammering atoms obliterates my stupor. The acute percussion of water on my skin electrifies my senses into the present. It speaks an unexpected language. The language of joy.

Could it be? No.

I have promised never again to feel that; but it is joy, in some embryonic form. I recognize it as I would recognize a relative's face gazing out from the amber of an old, faded photograph. Someone I have never met, someone dead a hundred years before my own conception. Someone carrying my bloodline forward from the deep past. I recognize the gaze, the way the eyes observe the world with a stern determination to understand, the way the nose is too straight, and the mouth slightly curves as if smiling but not quite smiling. This is familiar.

I stare out into the noise and chaos of rain. I remember my therapist saying that eventually I'll still feel the pain but from a greater distance, like I've walked further down the road and the music is more faint. Still the same music, but not so brutally loud.

In my mind, I listen to your lullaby tinkling softly from the windup mobile of moons and stars that used to spin above your angelic face. I want to run to you.

I drift in and out of abstract dreams, shallow ditches of muddy water. I wake up all through the night. In the dark, I walk to where your crib stood. I stand there until I am so cold that I feel as close to you as I can be.

My arm is still reaching out into the cold storm. I am numb. I curl my fingers to cup the battering of water into my palm. I watch the frigid liquid run out between my fingers. I can't hold this.

My phone rings downstairs, playing that cheerful marimba riff I keep meaning to change. I don't want to talk. I don't want to say hello, as if the world is all in order. It's probably just a telemarketer who'll mispronounce my name. If I answer, I'll just stand there, saying nothing.

Yesterday, I packed your clothes and donated them to the women's clinic. They smelled like soap and sun.

Driving home, I looked out through my tears at the traffic and wondered how I could be driving, if I even should be driving. It was like being in two places at once. In the car, turning corners, winding up the canyon, driving up the dirt road to the house; but also not in the car, somewhere far away, a puzzle of emotions, an excavation site all dug up and scattered.

Why did I give away your clothes? Someone told me it would make me feel better, that having them around was making me crazy. I saved a few things: your yellow romper, your terry cloth jumpsuit, the Piglet rattle, and the quilted baby blanket my mother made from scraps of my childhood dresses.

The rain is passing now, down the canyon. A blinding glare of sunlight pushes the storm eastward towards Boulder. Perhaps there will be a rainbow.

Once, there was a rainbow stretching from one end of the canyon all the way to the other. I stood on the front deck for an hour just staring, waiting for it to fade. It didn't. Finally, I went back into the house, even though all that color was still out there. How much beauty can a person absorb all at once? How much sadness?

I pull myself back into my cocoon, away from the open threshold. I reach for the door and slide it closed against the chill wind that has picked up in the rain's wake. Through the wet glass the world looks blurred.

Maybe I'll go downstairs and check my voicemail. There might be a message. Maybe I'll make myself some hot tea, do whatever it takes to keep moving, to fall under the force of habit like a gravity pulling me into my life again.

I should go out for a walk in the fresh stinging air. I don't want to. I want to curl up in bed and make myself very small.

Very small, like you were when you were here; so small I could almost hold you with one hand. Your heart was fragile, a tiny bird fluttering, flying away.

On the Mother Road to Father

Sophie pulls off of Interstate 40 and drives into the eastern edge of Albuquerque. It's late afternoon on a Friday.

Bad timing, but she overslept in Oklahoma City. She wants to take Central Avenue, the actual Route 66 through the city. According to her GPS, taking Central will take about the same amount of time as staying on the freeway, so why not take the scenic route?

As it turns out, Central is not so scenic. It's gritty, lined with fast food chains, car parts and towing businesses, plus a few box stores. Still, she has the top down on the convertible and is traveling in style along the historic stretch.

There are still a few iconic Route 66 motels. Most are in bad shape. Some are open for business, though she's not sure the business they're open for is legal.

Sophie is making the time-honored trip on the Mother Road, driving Route 66 from Chicago to Santa Monica, all 2137 miles. The original Route 66 is mostly paved over by Interstate 40, but in some places you can drive the original roadway for short stretches, as she's doing now.

She's driving a mint-condition 1959 Cadillac Series 62 in the original pink with a white leather interior. She calls the car Marilyn, because it's both innocent and seductive. She and Marilyn have received a lot of cat calls, whistles and outright applause on this trip. The attention makes her a bit anxious, but it's also a treat. She's an entertainment lawyer and usually her clients are the ones getting all of the attention.

She is soaking in the temporary glamour. Albuquerque is especially smitten by the car. The city still honors its Route 66 heritage, some Mother Road landmarks here have been renovated and reopened as burger joints and motels.

In thirty minutes, she reaches the city's old downtown and traffic comes to a full stop. She's essentially double-parked in front of the renovated Art Deco KiMo theater. The theater's entrance vestibule is painted with Southwest style murals. The marque reads, *Easy Rider.* How appropriate. Maybe she should park the car and go watch the film. After all, it depicts a road trip on Route 66, though based on very different motivations from her own.

At the moment, she's behind a Chevy Impala lowrider tricked out with a blue glitter finish and high-gloss chrome. Luckily, the driver prefers old school to rap and the Supremes are singing their soulful MoTown hit, *Stop in the Name of Love!* Also appropriate, as everyone is stopped, though not in the name of love as there is a lot of impatient honking going on.

The exhaust from the Chevy is noxious. She considers putting up the vinyl top, but better to just let the exhaust clear with the breeze. She's trying to keep the top down as much as possible, after all that's the experience this car was designed to provide, even though for her it means wearing SPF 100 on her face and neck. The sun is not her friend. She never gets a tan, just a burn. She's wearing a long-sleeved white shirt and has a white scarf wrapped over her head and around her neck, a la Sophia Loren, after whom she is named, though she now prefers Sophie. As far as she knows, there is no Italian in her heritage, just English, Irish and a touch of Norwegian.

An eight-cylinder Cadillac is not an economic choice for this mega trip. It's costing her a fortune in high octane gas, but Marilyn is the reason Sophie is taking the trip in the first place.

The convertible is actually quite a comfortable ride at a decent speed. The large windshield keeps her out of the wind, with just a slight cooling draft from the sides. Right now, however, Sophie feels like she's sitting in a solar oven and it's only April.

She could decide to stay in Albuquerque tonight. She's put in over eight hours of driving already, but she has a reservation at the Hotel El Rancho in Gallup and doesn't want to miss staying there. The historic Route 66 hotel has an emotional connection for her. She'll still get there before dark, a two-hour drive into the sunset through a thoroughly southwestern landscape of mesas and sandstone cliffs.

Finally, Sophie's rolling out of the city limits and is back on I-40. At first there's not much to see. A lot of barren open space, then a big casino, then a lot more barren open space. About an hour from Gallup there are massive rust-colored cliffs off to the right. She feels like a movie star, a very tired one, and she knows all about very tired movie stars!

She pulls into the El Rancho's parking lot just after seven. She puts up the vinyl top, rolls up the windows, locks the car and turns on the alarm. She worries about Marilyn at night so far from home in these places with dubious reputations.

Sophie checks in and then heads for the hotel restaurant. She orders a steak dinner with a baked potato and salad, plus a Michelob Ultra in a tall frosty glass.

Many movie stars stayed at the Hotel El Rancho while filming or traveling in the southwest. Their signed, framed photos adorn the walls. Their names are a who's who of Hollywood greats. John Wayne, May West, Gregory Peck, Jane Fonda, Katharine Hepburn, Kirk Douglas, even Ronald Reagan, the list goes on. Sophie will stay in a room that was a favorite of Doris Day's.

The lobby is opulent in an old west kitschy kind of way with a huge chandelier made of three wagon wheels, plush brocade covered furniture fit for a bordello and lots of Navajo rugs. Her dad used to love staying here, so she wants to experience it.

She doesn't sleep soundly. The room smells musty with age and the sheets have a bit too much lavender linen spray. Still, it's good to know her dad slept in this very room.

She gets up early and eats in the hotel restaurant, over-priced but convenient.

She has only six and a half hours of driving today to get to Kingman, Arizona, where she'll stay at a Holiday Inn. Then on to Santa Monica, another seven or eight hours depending on the traffic once she approaches Los Angeles.

Once in Santa Monica, where Route 66 ends, she'll stay with her dad's partner, Antonio, at the beach house for a few days. She and Antonio have a discreet plan to give some of her dad's ashes a sendoff from the end of the Santa Monica Pier at sunset. Her dad had loved watching sunsets from that spot, so it seems like something he'd have wanted.

He passed away three months ago from the lung cancer he'd fought valiantly, and at times not so valiantly, for almost two years. She'd flown out to see him for a long weekend once a month all during that last year, and then one more time for his funeral.

Her dad gave her the Cadillac for her 21st birthday, twenty years ago. In part, she was sure, as an apology. He'd left her mom when

Sophie was fourteen to go live in Los Angeles, pursuing his dream of acting and living openly as a gay man. It had taken Sophie a long, long time to begin to forgive him. She wasn't completely there yet, but her heart was mostly mended. She'd started watching his films about ten years ago. She'd watched his best film, *Thunderbird,* over and over in the past three months, ending up in tears each time. He received an Oscar for his role as Jason Thunderbird in that film, well deserved, she thought. Thunderbird had become his nickname and, for her, a personal term of endearment she cherishes.

Sophie also cherishes his ridiculously expensive to maintain Cadillac Series 62 all these years. She takes good care of the vintage car, but now only uses Marilyn on special occasions, and for Sunday drives when she has the leisure time, which isn't often enough.

Over the past two years, Sophie has acquired a deep respect for Antonio, after seeing his fastidious and loving care for her dad during his cancer treatments and hospice time. She is giving Marilyn to Antonio. Santa Monica is the perfect home for the car. Marilyn will help Antonio with his grief. Driving in this luxurious automobile is like having a day spa treatment. He needed that! Antonio was still a knockout at age sixty-four. A flamboyant gay Italian man in a pink Cadillac convertible will definitely turn heads, and that will be good for him too. She'll fly home knowing Marilyn will be well-loved, well-maintained, and taken out for a spin on a regular basis. That makes her happy, even though she'll miss Marilyn.

So, this trip is their last adventure together and Sophie is savoring every minute.

She puts the top down before starting the next part of her journey, to experience the vast Arizona views without impediment, though it is quite chilly. She's glad to be wearing her dad's leather bomber jacket, another and more recent gift. She's checked the weather forecast. It claims there might be snow, but she doesn't believe it. The sky is blue with only light wispy clouds.

Back on the highway, she can see a dark cloud bank off to the north, but it looks to be at least a hundred miles away. She turns up the volume on her iTunes playlist of Nat King Cole, her dad's favorite, and starts singing along.

If you ever plan to motor west. Travel my way, take the highway that's the best. Get your kicks on Route 66.

Driving the Mother Road through northern Arizona is like being in a western film. She hasn't seen this part of the country since she drove

Marilyn from Santa Monica to Saint Louis twenty years ago, where she lived with her mom at the time. That was the most outrageous adventure she'd ever had, and it remains so to this day.

After driving for two hours on the expansive landscape of the Colorado Plateau with its low desert brush and endless vistas, she stops at the Petrified Forest National Park. She raises the top on Marilyn, locks her up and goes to use the facilities.

Afterwards, she gazes out over the orange, mauve and white mounds of eroded sandstone dotted with huge petrified tree trunks the size of redwoods. It's an otherworldly place, a perfect set for a Sci Fi film.

The wind is kicking up and the temperature is dropping fast. She pulls up the collar of her jacket and heads back to the car. That dark cloud bank to the north is getting closer by the minute.

She keeps the top up, gets back on the road and turns on the heater. Twenty-minutes later, passing through Holbrook, the dark cloud arrives overhead.

Snow begins to fall in a dense curtain. The forecast was on target. She's used to driving in snow. Chicago has fierce winter storms, but she's never driven Marilyn in that kind of weather.

She's glad she has antifreeze in the radiator and wiper fluid. She's still about twenty miles from Winslow, where she plans to stop for lunch at the La Posada Hotel which has a renovated Harvey House restaurant, an historic landmark. She can wait out the storm there.

If it doesn't clear, and it only seems to be getting worse, she'll cancel her reservation in Kingman and stay at the La Posada. Hopefully, they'll have a room available.

Up ahead there is a dark movement on the side of the highway, barely visible through the densely falling snow.

Someone is walking out there!

Sophie is already driving fairly slowly, but slows even more. The walker is small and wrapped up in a brown blanket.

There is a wide dirt shoulder, so Sophie carefully pulls off of the road and parks. In her rearview mirror, she can see the tiny figure, who will surely freeze to death if Sophie doesn't help.

She zips up her bomber jacket, pulls on her wool beanie, leaves the engine running and goes out into the storm.

Walking towards the figure, who is wobbling slowly in her direction, she can see it is an elderly Navajo woman struggling against the storm. The wind is howling too loudly for conversation.

Sophie gestures towards the car and the two of them walk slowly to the Cadillac. Sophie helps the woman into the passenger seat. By the time Sophie gets back behind the wheel, the old woman appears to be dead.

Good Lord! Sophie thinks. *Please don't let her be dead!*

She's relieved to hear the woman's raspy breath returning. She isn't dead, just asleep. She must be exhausted. The dark brown blanket over her shoulders is soaked from the snow. Sophie carefully removes it and places it on the floorboard in front of the woman's feet, where the heating vent will dry it. She takes off her bomber jacket and lays it gently over the tiny figure. She has to run the defroster with the air conditioner on for a few minutes to defog the windshield. Once it is clear, she puts on her left-turn signal. She doesn't see any headlights in the snow behind her and is able to get safely back onto the highway.

She turns the heater back on full blast, worried about the woman next to her.

"Hang in there, Grandma," she whispers. "We're almost there."

The first signs for Winslow begin to appear. It's not a big town. Her GPS leads her to the La Posada Hotel, which is on the business loop of I-40, the old Highway 66.

When she stops under the overhang in front of the lobby, the slight jerk forward wakes up her passenger, who turns to her and smiles, with a few missing teeth.

"Do you understand English?" Sophie asks.

The woman just smiles. Apparently not.

"We are going inside now," Sophie says, pointing to the hotel entrance and then to the woman and to herself. She feels foolish. Of course they are going inside, why else would they be parked here.

The woman hands the jacket back to Sophie.

Sophie checks the blanket on the floorboard. It's dry and warm. She drapes it over the woman's shoulders, puts on her jacket, grabs her purse and gets out of the car. She'll take the woman inside first and then park Marilyn in the lot.

The lobby is toasty. There's a fire going in a massive fireplace.

Sophie leads the woman to a leather couch facing the flames and has her sit down.

"I'll be right back," she says.

She has a sudden revelation. There's a translation app on her phone. She looks to see if it has Navajo.

No such luck.

After parking the car, Sophie is glad to see that the woman is still on the couch. She appears to be sleeping again.

Sophie walks up the lobby's entrance of the Harvey House restaurant. The young male host looks Native American.

"Hi there," she says. "I have a sort of odd question and I'm hoping you can help me. Plus, I want a table for lunch as well, for two."

"Sure," he says.

"I picked up an elderly woman who was walking along the highway in this snowstorm about fifteen miles from here. She doesn't seem to understand or speak English. I'd like to buy her lunch and then I'll need to figure out what best to do for her after that. I'm worried about her."

The young man looks into the lobby at the couch.

"Oh, that's Susie Roundhouse!" he says, without a hint of surprise. "She likes to go to the post office."

"Really? From where? She was walking miles from anywhere."

"Yeah. She lives in a hogan on the Rez. Not in town."

"She walks along the highway frequently?"

"Someone always picks her up." He chuckles. "Hitching is the official Navajo bus service."

"Do you speak Navajo?" she asks.

"Yes. I'll talk with her. I know her grandson too. Lives close. We can call him."

"That will be terrific! I'd like to get her something to eat first though. Will she let me take her out for lunch here in the restaurant, do you think?"

He smiles and nods.

"My name is Sophie, by the way," she says.

"Nate."

Back at the couch, Nate talks with Susie in the soft, halting language of the Diné people. It sounds gentle.

Susie nods her head and smiles up at Sophie.

Nate brings them to a table near another fireplace inside the restaurant, where they would be warm.

"What do you think she'll want to eat?" Sophie asks.

"Burger and fries," Nate says.

"Okay, great. Please bring us each a burger with fries. What about to drink, for her?"

"Coca Cola," he says.

"Fine, and I'll have a coffee, please."

Susie loves the burger and fries. She keeps saying something in Navajo every few bites. Maybe it's thank you, or maybe it's just yum.

The food is excellent. Sophie doubts the old woman will be able to finish the huge burger and generous portion of steak cut fries, but the tiny grandmother eats every last bite of the meal.

After paying the check and leaving a large tip for Nate, the two of them head back to the couch in the lobby. They have the space to themselves.

Nate has called Susie's grandson, Ike, who is on the way.

Susie looks much revived and has a twinkle in her eyes now. They sit in silence and wait, watching the flames.

Ike arrives and Susie's face lights up. She obviously loves the big burly Navajo man who is forever going to be her little grandson.

Ike apologizes, hopes his grandmother has not caused any trouble.

"Oh, no trouble," Sophie says. "I'm just so grateful I happened to be driving that way and could help her get here safely."

"So you gave Grammy lunch here," he said. "Very nice place. Thank you."

Sophie smiles. "It was my pleasure."

Susie says something to Ike in Navajo.

"She says burger and fries much better than at McDonald's."

"Please tell her I enjoyed our time together, and that I am happy she is safe with her grandson now."

Ike says something in Navajo, much too short to be what Sophie said.

"She says thank you. Wants to give you something."

"Oh, she doesn't need to give me anything."

What could this old woman possibly give her? Sophie wonders. She has nothing.

Susie says something to Ike while pointing to the back of her neck. Ike reached behind Susie's head. Susie chuckles, as if Ike is tickling her. She reaches under her shawl blanket and pulls something out from underneath. Then she reaches out her hand to Sophie, speaking in Navajo.

"She says Great Spirit tell her to give this to you. Keep your father close to your heart."

Sophie reaches out her hand, taking Susie's gift.

She gasps when she sees what it is, a silver pendant on a silver chain. The pendant is a thunderbird!

A thunderbird!

True, that is not an unusual symbol in the Southwest, but how could Susie know that it is, for Sophie, a symbol of her dad?

Susie chuckles again and says something to Sophie.

"She says put it on and you will feel better. No more sadness. Your papa is with you, very close."

The tears come then, Sophie can't stop them. Doesn't even want to stop them.

"Thank you, Susie!" she says. "Thank you!"

Her gratitude needs no translation. Susie understands, nods.

Sophie wants to embrace this frail old woman with all of her heart, but she knows this was not the Navajo way. She just nods back, with reverence.

"Gonna take her to my place now. Storm's getting bad," Ike says.

Sophie nods again. Susie nods again. They both smile their goodbyes.

Then Ike and Susie are out the door and getting into an old pickup parked under the overhang. They drive away into the swirling snow.

Sophie sits on the couch for a long time, her right hand over the thunderbird, which is hanging over her heart. She doesn't feel sad or angry any more. The heaviness that plagued her is gone.

She feels a rising wave of joy, a wellspring of love.

Follow the Raven

The old woman stood in the piñon forest, singing softly in her ancient language. She was not visible to the material world, only the ravens circling overhead felt her presence and cawed softly.

Sean ran along the winding mountain trail. He could see the city of Santa Fe stretched below with its tawny adobe buildings and old Spanish streets.

The fresh scent of juniper, piñon and cedar filled the air. Sean breathed deeply and felt grateful to be spending a week here, teaching yoga and meditation at the Ananda Zen Center.

His long blonde dreadlocks were tied in a ponytail and his Guatemalan textile backpack bounced jauntily on his shoulders.

Sean felt light-headed but his legs weren't letting him down. He lived in a beach town at sea level, so running at seven-thousand feet without getting winded was a pleasant surprise.

The old woman stepped onto the trail, making herself visible to the material world.

Sean ran around a horseshoe bend, lost in thought.

"Whoa!" he shouted, jumping into the brush to avoid running into an old woman who was standing in the middle of the trail. The rough chamisa brush scratched his bare legs and the rocky terrain made him stumble.

He felt the woman's hand grab his arm. She had a surprisingly strong grip. He found secure footing again on the decomposed granite. The old woman was still tightly holding his arm.

He stared at her in disbelief. She was no ordinary trail hiker. She looked ancient. Her face was painted white. There were thin vertical red lines painted from her forehead to her cheeks, which had two perfect red circles of thick rouge. Black braids came out from under her small feathered cap, a fox stole was draped around her neck, and a buckskin cape hung over her shoulders. In her right hand she held a raw blue corn cob.

Her opalescent eyes scrutinized him, making him nervous.

How did she get here? It was not an easy climb from the trailhead.

Suddenly, she laughed. Then, she hit him in the chest with the corn cob, so hard that had she not still been holding onto his arm, the force could have toppled him.

"Hey!" he shouted.

He tried to wrestle free from her grip, but she was ridiculously strong.

She smiled at him with a sparkle in her eyes.

"Follow deeee raven," she said, with an accent he couldn't place.

She let go of his arm, and with deer-like agility, ran through the brush into the forest.

In moments, she was gone.

Sean felt dizzy and sat down on the ground. What just happened?

He removed his pack and found his cell phone. No bars, but the time on the clock shocked him. It was 4:46. He'd left the center right after morning meditation, probably no later than 10:00. That was almost seven hours ago.

He got up and walked back in the direction of the trailhead. The sun sank behind the ridge top, leaving him in shadow. It was getting cold. He started to run. It only took him forty-five minutes to reach the trailhead, then another fifteen minutes to get to the Ananda Zen Center.

He was missing about five hours of time. What had happened to it? More importantly, what had happened *during* it?

He needed to sit and process. Alone in the meditation hall, he was unable to shake a deep sense of impending, something. He wasn't sure exactly what, but it wasn't ominous, just the pressing of questions reaching for answers.

He meditated for a while to quiet down his active mind. Then he walked back to his bed and breakfast along the road in the sunset light.

In the casita's small bedroom, he kicked off his shoes and plopped onto the futon. He pulled the down comforter over him and stared at the glow in the dark stars glued to the ceiling.

He awakened to morning sunlight on his face. He'd slept through the night.

He took a hot shower and decided to shave. The small bathroom mirror was fogged over with steam. He wiped it down with a hand towel and caught sight of his bare chest in the reflection above the sink.

There was something on his chest, above his heart, exactly where the old woman had hit him. He'd just showered, why was there a black smudge still on his skin? He leaned in closer to the mirror. The image wasn't clear. He wiped away the steam again. The black smudge on his chest was no smudge. It was a tattoo of a bird in flight, a raven.

Then, just for an instant, he swore he saw the old woman's reflection in the foggy glass. She was standing just behind him. He turned quickly, but she was gone.

Had he imagined her? He looked at the raven tattoo. It was no illusion. It was real.

He got dressed, found his cell phone and called his work associate Jennie in Santa Cruz. He'd meant to check in with her last night but had fallen asleep. Jennie was teaching his classes at Gaia Yoga Flow while he was here. She was a dynamite instructor. People loved her.

She answered on the second ring. It was good to hear her bubbly voice. She was always in a cheerful mood. She assured him that all was well at Gaia Yoga Flow, and that everyone missed him and sent their love.

He didn't tell her about his weird experience on the trail yesterday. It was too disturbing, though not telling her was a challenge. It was the biggest thing on his mind.

After the call, Sean left the casita and headed down the garden path to the kitchen door of the main house, where his complimentary breakfast would be waiting. The host, Karen, left the kitchen door unlocked for him.

This morning, she'd baked banana bread and was still in the kitchen herself. Sean ate two warm slices of the bread and sipped a cup of Darjeeling tea.

He liked Karen. She was a retired elementary school teacher in her early seventies. They had a jovial, easy energy together, which made staying at her place very comfortable.

Born and raised in Santa Fe, Karen was an excellent resource on all things local. She'd chuckled when Sean told her, on the first morning of his stay, that he'd taken a nice walk by the creek.

"That, my dear," she'd said, "is the Santa Fe *River.*"

The trickle of water would hardly qualify as a creek in California, but in the desert, it was precious water worthy of being called a river.

"Are you teaching yoga classes today," Karen asked, "or do you have some time to explore?"

"Time to explore," he said, "but on foot. Anything on the Santa Fe Plaza you'd recommend?"

"Well, the La Fonda Hotel is a gorgeous restored adobe. It's one of only three remaining historic Harvey Houses from the mid-eighteen hundreds. Go visit the Cathedral Basilica of Saint Francis of Assisi. I know, that's a mouthful, right? It was built in the late 1800s. Beautiful light in there. If you get hungry, the food cart on the Plaza right across from the Five and Dime has fresh tamales. I highly recommend them!"

"Perfect. Thanks."

"Oh, and do visit with the Navajo and Zuni vendors who sit in front of the Palace of the Governors, it's the oldest building in Santa Fe. You can't miss them. They always gather a crowd. Their wares are certified handmade. My favorite shop, Mudhead, also sells authentic Native American goods. Fun to look around in there. Walk down La Vereda, turn right onto E. Palace. The shop is just before you get to the Plaza."

"Super. Thanks."

"I'm off to the farmer's market this morning," she said. "Have a blast."

Sean washed his mug and dish then went back to the casita to prepare for his day.

He wanted to buy a gift for Jennie to thank her for teaching his classes. He was also going to look for anything related to a raven. The old woman had told him emphatically to "follow the raven." That was pretty cryptic advice. He had no idea what it meant, but if he was supposed to follow a raven, he'd have to find one first.

The morning was sunny and brisk. Perfect for a walking tour of the center of town. He grabbed his light wool jacket.

He decided to start by visiting the vendors in front of the Palace of the Governors. He moved along slowly with the mass of tourists gathered there under the portico. The jewelry was laid out on rugs at the feet of the artisans. There were at least thirty vendors and the jewelry was exquisite. He didn't see any ravens. When he noticed a silver pendant with a turquoise inlay turtle, he knew he'd found the perfect gift for Jennie. She adored turtles. He bought the necklace from the elderly Navajo woman. She spoke no English but gave him a gentle smile and nod.

He wandered all around the busy Plaza, listened for a while to a talented jazz guitarist playing on a bench. He dropped some money into the guy's opened case. He walked to the cathedral. The front entrance had two massive wooden doors ornately carved with saints. He opened one of them. It was at least twelve feet high and maybe five inches thick. Heavy and substantial. You had to step into awareness to enter this church.

He sat in a pew, enjoying the silence. The tall stained windows filtered a cheerful light into the massive space. The murals painted inside the domed ceiling depicted heavenly scenes. He said a prayer for guidance.

Then he went back out into the sun, crossed the street and entered the La Fonda Hotel on the corner. It was somber inside, lots of Spanish colonial style furniture. He looked around for a raven, but only found a lot of Texans hanging out in the lobby. He went back out into the sun.

In all of his wanderings, he hadn't seen a single raven, except for a ratty old bird who was picking through a garbage can on the Plaza. Following *that* raven made no sense at all.

He bought a cheese and green pepper tamale from the food cart. It was muy picante! He drank an iced tea to cool off his mouth.

He walked back to E. Palace and found Mudhead. Strange name, he thought. The shop smelled of cedar incense. It was jam packed with Native American art, relics, jewelry, and books on the Southwest. There were three rooms. In the one furthest back, he spotted her as soon as he walked in.

She was small, maybe eight inches tall. He went over and stood transfixed. It was definitely the old woman!

The wooden carved figure was standing behind glass in a locked case. She had a white face with vertical thin red lines and round red cheeks. She wore a light brown cape and a cap with feathers on top of her head. In her left hand, she held a corn cob.

He was perplexed. How was this possible?

The case had a sign that read, "Hopi Kachina Dolls."

"Would you like to see something in this case?" a friendly voice said from behind him.

He was momentarily startled.

"Um, yes. Very much," he said. "This one here." He pointed.

"Oh, good choice."

She unlocked the case and pulled out the small wooden painted doll.

"Do you know anything about Kachinas?" she asked.

"No," he said. "What can you tell me about this one?"

"She is a Grandmother Kachina, also known as the Mother of all Katsinam and as Mother Earth. She is a spirit guide who protects children and she can be quite fierce about it."

Sean could see that fierceness in the doll's face. No smile, although her eyes looked kind.

"Does she always appear like this?" he asked. "The white face with the red lines. The corn cob in her right hand?"

"Yes, that's her traditional appearance."

"I'm amazed I've never heard about these," Sean said.

"The Hopi are a very private culture. Outside of the Southwest, very few people know about them or any of the pueblo cultures. In fact, here in New Mexico, up until the mid 1970's, holding sacred dances at the pueblos was illegal. Can you believe that?"

"That's just awful. The 1970s. Really?"

"So much for progressive thinking in the twentieth century, right?"

"Are the Kachinas part of those sacred dances?"

"Yes. Very much so."

"But it's okay for a non-native person to own a Kachina doll?"

"Oh, sure. The dolls are considered pieces of art. We buy them directly from the Hopi carvers, and have strong relationships with them."

"That's great. What's the price of this one?"

"She's $300, which is a very good price for the exquisite detail."

"I believe it, but I'm afraid that's out of my price range. I do appreciate your taking the time to enlighten me. Do you have any books about Hopi Kachinas, or the belief system around them?" Sean asked.

"I'd recommend "Book of the Hopi" by Frank Waters. That's a great resource, very thorough. Waters actually lived with the Hopi. I believe we may even have a paperback copy. I think it's about $17.00."

"Now that's in my price range. I'll take it, if you have it."

While the sales clerk went to find the book, Sean took a photo of the Grandmother Kachina doll with his phone. He wished he had the money. He really wanted to take it home, but the photo would have to do.

Finding this Grandmother Kachina was an elegance of chance. What were the odds? Now he had a context for his experience. Was the old woman who appeared on the trail an actual Grandmother Kachina? He doubted a Hopi spirit guide had come to visit him. There didn't seem any rhyme or reason in that. He was just Sean, an ordinary guy. Then again, the world was a mysterious place filled with unexplained phenomena, and they did call New Mexico the *Land of Enchantment.* So, who knew?

Book and turtle necklace safely stashed in his backpack, Sean headed back to the casita.

Cars passed on the street. He didn't pay much attention to them, until a red Mini Cooper drove by. It had a local New Mexico license plate. Personalized. "D RAVEN."

He stood stunned for a moment, then began to run up the sidewalk after the car. The sidewalk was made of uneven old bricks, not an easy surface for running. He got into the street where he could run faster. The Mini Cooper turned right a few blocks ahead of him. He sprinted, not wanting to lose sight of it.

Turning the corner, he slowed down. The Mini Cooper had pulled over and parked. The driver was getting out. Sean stood still and waited.

The driver was a small woman with long black hair. Raven hair. She put on a jacket, grabbed a large black bag from the car, swung it over her shoulder and headed further down the street. He followed at a discreet distance. She crossed over the next street and then started walking south along the Santa Fe River.

"Follow D RAVEN," he thought to himself. Well, it was the only raven he'd encountered so far.

He followed her. She turned left and then took another left onto Canyon Road, where the world-class art galleries were located. She walked fast with a determined gait. She didn't go into any of the galleries she passed.

Finally, she entered a sculpture gallery.

Sean waited a few minutes, then went inside. She was standing towards the back with a tall, heavy set man who was talking to her.

"Thanks again for coming in on such short notice. Go ahead and take tomorrow off to compensate. I've gotta run."

The man, her boss Sean assumed, pulled on an overcoat and headed out the door.

That meant Sean could have a private conversation with D RAVEN, if he could figure out how to approach her and what to say.

He was starting to feel like he was in a mystery novel or a Bond film.

She looked over to him. "Let me know if you have any questions," she said. He detected a slight Irish accent.

"Sure, thanks."

Sean wandered through the gallery. There was a massive infinity symbol carved from a solid piece of white marble for $80,000. Talk about not in his price range.

He walked up to the sales desk.

"Hi," he said.

"Hello. Did you see something you're interested in?"

She had taken off her jacket and was wearing a fairly low-cut dress. As she turned towards him, he could see a small tattoo on her upper chest. It was a raven in flight.

"Whoa," he involuntarily whispered.

"Are you okay? Feeling faint? The altitude can do that," she said, kindly. "Would you like some water. Easy to get dehydrated too, even though it's not hot out. Especially if you've been running," she added, then flashed him a coy smile.

He was found out. She'd seen him running after her car.

"Water would be terrific. Thank you."

"I'll be right back. You're not the first person to get light-headed."

Now what? Could he ask her about the tattoo? That seemed a bit forward.

She returned with water in an actual glass. Classy gallery.

"Thank you," he said.

He drank all of the water, gave her the empty glass, took a deep breath and jumped in.

"That's an amazing tattoo," he said.

"Oh," she said, seeming a bit taken aback. "It's my name. Raven. Deirdre Raven, but my friends call me Raven."

"Bond. James Bond, but my friends call me Sean."

"Sean Connery?" she asked.

There was that coy smile again. She was a quick wit. He liked that.

"Ha! No." he said, sheepishly. "Um, Sean Warren."

"Well, Sean. Are you a fan of sculpture?"

"A fan, yes, but unfortunately for you, not in the market to buy anything today."

"Most of our sales happen through other avenues. The gallery is mostly a showcase. I am well aware that the tourists who wander in here are not exactly in the market to pick up something that weighs four tons."

There was that wit again. Sean relaxed a bit.

"Your first visit to Santa Fe?" she asked.

"Yes."

"Vacation?"

"No, teaching a yoga and meditation workshop at the Ananda Zen Center."

"Oh, fantastic! I've been meaning to go there."

He wanted to return the conversation to the tattoo, but how.

"So, Miss Raven,"

"Just Raven."

"Okay, just Raven, if you don't mind my asking, where did you get that incredible tattoo? A local artist?"

Raven frowned for a moment, giving him a look he couldn't read.

"Yes, local." She blushed. "I don't think they are available anymore."

"You mean the shop closed down?"

"Not exactly."

"Never mind, I'm sorry."

Follow D RAVEN, his mind insisted. You can't just let this go. He cleared his throat, then launched back in.

"This is going to sound a little strange," he said, "well, more than a little strange actually, but I need to tell you something."

"Okay," Raven said, a worried look casting a shadow over her bright demeanor.

"I have a tattoo exactly like yours."

Now Sean had the worried look. How would she react to that piece of news?

"*Exactly?*" she asked.

"*Exactly*, and in the same place."

"Hold on," she said. She looked around the gallery. They were the only ones inside. She walked to the door and turned the OPEN sign to CLOSED, then came back to him.

"I'd prefer not to get interrupted by a bunch of tourists," she said. "This is too important. Would you be willing to show me your tattoo?"

"Sure."

Sean unzipped his coat and lowered the collar on his t-shirt.

She stared at his tattoo. "I take it you didn't get yours at a tattoo parlor either."

"Nope."

"How long ago?

"Yesterday."

"Oh, wow! That's recent. Two months ago for me."

Sean pulled out his cellphone, found the photo of the Grandmother Kachina from Mudhead and showed it to Raven.

"Are you codding me?"

"Not sure what codding is," Sean said, "but I'm sure I'm not. She appeared out of nowhere on a trail where I was running."

"I was up in the forest too when she came to me. What does it mean?" Raven asked.

"I was hoping you could tell me!"

"I have no idea."

"Did she say anything to you?" Sean asked.

"Yes, but it was cryptic. Go to canyon."

"I was told, follow the raven, but she pronounced it, deeee raven.

"That's why you were following me! You saw my license plate!"

"Bingo!"

"I saw you running back there. Just thought you'd just picked a lousy place to jog. Then, I saw you walking behind me, but thought you were just going to Canyon Road like every other tourist."

"So you took this job because it was on Canyon?"

"Yes. I have no idea why they hired me. I have zero experience working in a gallery and I'm not even an artist. I've mostly worked for day care centers. I have a Masters in Early Childhood Development, but there's been nothing available in my field."

"Hmm."

"What?"

"The Grandmother Kachina protects the children."

"So I've heard, and so do day care centers, right? I have pondered that connection, but she didn't tell me to work with children. She told me to work here."

"There are a lot of canyons around Santa Fe. Maybe she didn't mean Canyon Road."

"True, but this job landed in my lap through an unexpected connection. I really needed a job, in any case, so I took it. Now, here you are. Perhaps my taking this job was about the two of us meeting each other."

"Maybe. Seems like a stretch. Let me ask you one more thing," Sean said. "After you saw her, was there a bunch of missing time? I mean, was it like several hours had passed but you only remember a few minutes?"

"You too, huh? Yes. About five hours as a matter of fact. I still have no idea what happened during that missing time."

"Me neither. Though we both received a tattoo and that usually takes time. Then again, she hit me with her corn cob right over my heart. I think that's when the tattoo showed up, sort of instantaneously."

"She hit me too. It really hurt!"

"Do you think she took us on some sort of shamanic journey?" Sean pondered.

"It has occurred to me," Raven said, "but it's not like I remember anything."

"That makes two of us then."

"I really should reopen the gallery now. Are you free tomorrow? I just got the day off."

"The Zen center has an open meditation followed by a brunch every Sunday. It starts at 10:00. You could come. We can talk afterwards."

"Brilliant! Let's exchange phone numbers."

With Raven's number in his contact list, Sean left the gallery.

He wandered around on Canyon Road in a daze, his mind racing. At least there was someone with whom he could share the mystery, and hopefully solve it.

He spent the evening reading in *Book of the Hopi*.

The morning dawned clear and sunny. He showered, put on his nice clothes as he would be with all of the Ananda staff and community. He hoped Raven would follow through.

She was already seated in the meditation hall when he arrived. They exchanged smiles. After the meditation, everyone moved into the community hall where a spread of vegetarian foods was laid out. Sean and Raven filled their plates and found a bench.

"This is terrific," Raven said.

They ate in silence and after they were finished, Sean offered to take her plate and utensils to the kitchen.

"Thanks," Raven said.

"Hey, I need to mingle a bit," Sean said, "proper decorum and all, since it's my final day with the community here. Would you like to join me while I do that?"

"No, it's fine," Raven said. "I'll just look around and meet you back here in a while."

"Sounds good."

Sean talked with several people. It was a charming community. After about fifteen minutes, he rejoined Raven.

"Look what I found!" she said, triumphantly, leading him down a hallway to a bulletin board. She pointed to a flyer.

Sean read the announcement. "Seeking coordinator for new day care center opening at Ananda."

"It was just put up today. Look at the date stamp," Raven said.

"Wow!" He gave her an unplanned hug. "That's amazing! This is your job!"

"I sure hope so! I was just sort of looking at the board in a distracted way and then voila! There it was, my perfect job! A woman came over to me a few minutes ago. She noticed I was looking at the flyer and asked if I was interested. Her name is Carla. She's one of the center's directors. I'm coming in for an interview tomorrow afternoon!"

"Carla is wonderful, so is the other director, Joseph. I have a strong feeling you'll get this job, and if you do, then I think you'll have solved your mystery."

"But what about yours?"

"Maybe I was just the conduit for getting you here, so that you could protect the children."

"Perhaps, but I think there's more to it than that."

"I'm leaving the day after tomorrow, so if there's more to it, the more part needs to show up soon."

"I think it will," she said. "Wow! I'm all tingly inside! Thank you for inviting me here!"

"Serendipity!"

They went outside and sat in the garden.

Raven told Sean that she'd moved to Santa Fe from Seattle two years ago, looking to get away from the damp and grey. Too much like Ireland, she'd confided.

"Hey, I just realized something," Sean said. "We are in a canyon right here."

They looked around. The property went steeply up on both sides of the garden.

"You're right! That's perfect!" Raven said.

They sat for a while, soaking in the quiet beauty of the place.

Then Raven said she needed to go. She promised to call him after her interview and offered to drive him back to the B&B, but he wanted to stay at the center a while longer.

Sean went back to the meditation hall and sat in the silence.

He realized he wasn't feeling excited about going back to Santa Cruz. Maybe he could extend his stay here in Santa Fe, if the Ananda Center had anything to offer him longer term. Jennie was enjoying teaching his classes at Gaia Yoga Flow.

He'd been feeling restless at home for some time now, wanting to explore something different.

Could Santa Fe be that something different? After all, it even called itself, "The City Different."

When he got back to the casita, there was a note taped on his door. Karen was inviting him to have dinner. She'd cooked up a batch of her special chili and insisted he try it.

The chili was delicious. Their conversation was light-hearted as usual. Sean didn't tell Karen about his mysterious tattoo. He did tell her about the Grandmother Kachina doll he'd admired at Mudhead. She explained that Mudhead was the name of another Hopi Kachina, a clown figure. She owned two kachina dolls herself and showed them to him. One was an owl figure, quite large and foreboding.

"That one cost me more than I could afford," Karen said, "but isn't he magnificent! Looks like he could fly right off his wooden pedestal."

The other doll was a Grandmother, very small and in muted colors.

"This is my favorite," Karen said. "She keeps me honest with myself."

"What do you mean?"

"Well, whenever I am pulled away from my core principles or my truest dreams, she gives me that scrutinizing look as if to say, remember who you are! Then I do remember. I stop being a ninny and live up to my potential, as best as I can."

"I like that. That's good wisdom."

Sean lay in bed that night wondering about his own true potential. He couldn't imagine that teaching yoga and meditation to liberal elite Californians qualified as living up to his potential. How much did they really need him? Yoga and meditation were his passion, but wasn't there a way to promote them that would have a greater impact, make a bigger difference in the world?

He had a meeting with the directors at Ananda in the morning. Maybe he'd gain some clarity from that.

He'd done what the Grandmother Kachina had told him to do. He'd followed D RAVEN. Was connecting his new friend to the Zen center the end of it then? If so, why did it still feel incomplete?

He eventually dropped off to sleep.

His early morning meeting with Carla and Joseph was brief but potent. As a result of it, Sean's life was about to change dramatically.

Not only did they intend to hire Raven to coordinate their new day care center, they were also starting a new program of yoga and meditation for children and youth. They wanted Sean to be its director.

They were so impressed with his knowledge, energy and people skills, they felt he was the perfect choice for the position.

It was a dream job, and without even taking time to think it over, Sean had accepted their offer. He knew in his core it was the right decision.

Now he sat in the garden, on the same bench where he'd sat with Raven only yesterday. What a difference a day makes, as they say. With his life in a blender on high speed, he felt a little in shock.

His new job would begin in a month, allowing him plenty of time to give notice at Gaia Yoga Flow and prepare for the move. His new salary would be higher and the offer included a rent-free adobe casita on Ananda's peaceful grounds, for as long as he wanted to live there.

As if all of that wasn't enough of a windfall of blessings, they'd also given him a $300 bonus as enrollment in his workshop this week had been much higher than expected.

He knew exactly how he would spend the extra money, if Mudhead still had her!

Sean felt a wave of energy stream through his body as a revelation came to him. The raven tattoo was over his heart. Follow the raven. Follow your heart! It hadn't occurred to him until now, because until now, he hadn't really been following his heart.

It wasn't that he didn't enjoy teaching classes and workshops for adults, he did. He just never felt that it was his true calling. He saw teaching yoga and meditation to kids and youth as a chance to help shape their futures. Living in an increasingly stressful world filled with noise and chaos, they needed all the help they could get. Giving them tools for gaining self-awareness and inner peace would be a powerful contribution to their lives, and to his own. Sean felt an expansion in his heart, like the petals of a lotus flower opening.

He left the center and walked quickly down to Mudhead, filled with joy and anticipation.

When he reached the store, it was already crowded with tourists. He scooted around them and went directly into the back room.

He could see the glass case as soon as he entered.

Something was wrong. He walked up to the glass. His heart sank. There was an empty space where she had stood. She was gone.

Someone else had bought her!

He didn't want to believe it. Maybe they had moved the kachina to somewhere else in the store. Unlikely, but he had to ask.

The saleswoman who had talked with him on Saturday was not in the store today. A younger woman was at the register.

"Excuse me," he said. "I was here on Saturday and saw a Grandmother Kachina doll in the case in the back room. She isn't there this morning. Did she get sold?"

"I'm new here," the young woman said. "Can you describe it?"

Sean took out his phone and showed her the photo.

"Oh, I don't remember that one, but if it's not there, I guess it sold over the weekend."

"Is there any way to be sure?" Sean asked, not yet willing to give up hope.

"We do keep a log by artist of objects sold as they receive an additional commission. Do you know the artist?"

"No, sorry, I don't, just that he or she is a Hopi carver."

"Okay. I'll take a look.

The young woman pulled out a large notebook and leafed through it rather slowly while Sean stood at the register, shifting his weight from foot to foot.

"There was a kachina sale yesterday for $300. Was that the price?"

"Yes," Sean said, dejectedly. "Thanks for checking."

He should have bought her on Saturday. Hindsight was a waste of energy. He knew that, but couldn't help being disappointed and a bit angry with himself. Everything had lined up so serendipitously. He thought for sure the Grandmother Kachina doll was meant to be the perfect finale.

He walked slowly back up the hill to the B&B, trying his best to experience only the gratitude he felt for all of the awesome blessings coming his way. Still, he missed her.

When he entered through the garden gate, Karen was outside weeding.

"Hi, Sean! Good to see you. Your last day here. That was a fast week."

"It flew by," he said.

He would tell her his exciting news about the job at Ananda a little later. He wasn't ready to jump into it now.

"There's fresh lemonade in the fridge if you're thirsty," Karen said, "and when I got home from Tai Chi this morning, there was a package on the front porch with your name on it. I put it on the kitchen counter for you."

"Okay, thanks."

A package? Something from Ananda probably. No one else knew where he was staying.

Sean went into the kitchen and found a rectangular box wrapped in plain brown paper on which his name was written in an odd script. It was just his first name and it was misspelled. Not from Ananda then.

He removed the paper to reveal a white gift box with a small gold sticker on the lid. It said, "Mudhead, Santa Fe."

Could it be?

He lifted the box lid and pulled away the folded tissue paper. He stared in disbelief, which bloomed into delight.

The Grandmother Kachina doll was smiling up at him.

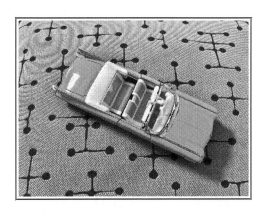

From the West Coast

Angel of the Lost and Found

Angela stared at the toe tag hanging out from the zipped body bag. It was a Jane Doe. Always a challenge. No place to start, no connections to follow. A young Jane Doe was particularly disheartening. No place to go except to this depressing dead end, having just started out in life.

Sometimes it was all too heavy, this peculiar work of hers. She was like Don Quixote, but instead of dreaming the impossible dream, she was solving the impossible puzzle.

She couldn't complain though, the Consortium paid her exceedingly well for taking on these lost causes. Without her interventions, the Jane and John Does would end up as nameless cold cases.

Having been abandoned as a baby, raised in an orphanage, and later in foster homes, Angela had a strong heart connection with finding names for the nameless.

She would never know the name her own mother might have given her, so she felt satisfaction every time she found the true name of a John or Jane Doe. At least they would not go to the grave without their identities, and their loved ones would not have to wonder endlessly about what had happened to them. That was a torturous existence. She was bringing the family the peace that comes with closure, even if it was not a happy ending.

Angela unzipped the body bag and instantly noticed the toenails. She held her own thumb next to Jane Doe's toes. The vibrant color was an exact match.

There was only one place in Los Angeles that used Funtastique Fuchsia, a patented nail color designed by her friend Jasón, the owner of Salón Funtastique de Rodeo. The pedicure was recent, the color fresh and unfaded. She had her first lead.

Angela took note of the woman's features. Very young, probably late teens. Not a wrinkle in her facial tissue. Caucasian, not very tanned, that was unusual for LA. Long, blonde hair, natural, no sign of dark roots. Also unusual for LA. The eyes were closed. The toe tag had the color listed as green. Interesting. The most uncommon eye color. Medium breasts, natural, no sign of implants. Again, unusual for LA. Very skinny. Not unusual for LA, but these thin arms and legs had little muscle definition. This girl wasn't a runner and didn't look like she'd worked out at a club a day in her life. That was most unusual for LA.

Jane Doe was stunning, even with her now ashen complexion. She would have made an impression with life still flushing her cheeks and animating her eyes.

Angela didn't see any apparent wounds or obvious broken bones. No red abrasion around the neck, so not strangled. No indication of blunt trauma, no tissue bruising. Maybe a knife wound in the back?

Footsteps out in the hallway arrested Angela's attention. It was after six. This section of the morgue officially closed at five, but for police business it remained accessible around the clock.

She quickly zipped up the body bag, silently pushed the metal tray back into the refrigerated bay and closed the locker door.

Time to skedaddle. Then again, she'd really like to hear what was about to transpire, in case it related to her Jane Doe, though if it was the actual autopsy, she'd have to bail.

Being a shapeshifter was helpful when you were a private eye without police credentials. While she wasn't interested in being an actual fly on the wall, that could seriously backfire, she did want to be something with eyes, preferably just two of them.

Angela shifted into the shape of a female field mouse. She climbed to the top of a shelving unit across from the refrigerated bays. She was up high enough to be hidden from anyone's view and had a perfect vantage point of the room below.

Two men entered the morgue. The shorter one had a large bald spot and wore a white lab coat, likely the coroner. The taller one had a military style crew cut and was an officer of the law.

"Well, let's take a look," Crew Cut said. "Not that it will do much good. No ID on this one, and no leads."

Angela smiled. He was probably there for the Jane Doe case. She was one step ahead of him already, but this wasn't a competition. She was here to help not to thwart or taunt, though the taunting was sometimes irresistible. The officers could be so dense at times.

Bald Spot opened the Jane Doe cold chamber and pulled out the metal drawer.

Angela had lucked out. There were over a dozen bodies in the morgue at any time. Crew Cut could have been interested in any one of those instead.

"Just let me know when you're finished," Bald Spot said. "I'll be in my office doing some paperwork."

"Sounds like fun."

"A lot less messy than my other obligations," Bald Spot said, then laughed.

The laugh sounded sinister, Angela thought. Then again, who goes into this line of work without some penchant for the macabre?

Crew Cut unzipped the body bag. He checked the body for obvious injuries or bruising. Then, he slowly rolled the body halfway over to take a look at the back, holding Jane by the shoulder in a surprisingly tender way. He didn't seem to find anything of note.

Had Jane been poisoned perhaps? Usually, that left a contorted, pained expression on the face of the deceased. Angela doubted that scenario. Jane looked remarkably peaceful. So, what was the cause of death? She'd really like to take a look at the death certificate. It was likely not yet filled out. The body would not go to autopsy until after the police department had their look.

Angela heard a slight scratching sound behind her. Shit, it was another mouse, and it was coming to check her out. It squeaked.

Crew Cut glanced around. Had he heard it?

How do you say shush to a mouse, Angela wondered. She let the other mouse come closer, and after it sniffed her, nose to nose, the other mouse seemed satisfied that she was no threat and ran off. Close call. At least it hadn't wanted to mate! This animal shapeshifting had way more hazards than the Consortium training academy was inclined to mention.

Angela returned her attention to the scene below.

Crew Cut had rolled Jane Doe onto her back again, and was now looking at her hands and fingers. He scraped a sample from under a fingernail and slipped it into a baggie. Then he stared at her toes.

Was he going to take note of the unusual toenail color? Unlikely. The average man had no inkling of the nuances of a good pedicure.

Crew Cut sighed deeply. He zipped up the bag and pushed Jane Doe back into her cold dark cave. Then he left the room.

Angela scampered down to the tiled floor and scurried across it towards the wall with the window, which didn't close effectively, leaving open a tiny crack at the corner. That's how she'd gotten into the room, in the shape of a small spider.

She shifted back into arachnid form, crawled up the wall and out of the window. She crawled down the outer wall and was in the parking lot. She looked around to be sure no one was in sight. Then she shifted back into her human form. Being a spider freaked her out, all those legs, but it was very convenient for getting in and out of buildings. She shook off her heebie-jeebies and walked down the block.

When she got to the car, she sighed. Talk about the most conspicuous vehicle possible for someone working undercover. Her own quiet silver Prius was in the shop for some mysterious computer chip failure, so she'd borrowed her colleague Ernesto's ride. It was a 1955 Cadillac Fleetwood, think Elvis, but tricked out with a hot pink makeover, low-rider suspension and black and white fuzzy dice hanging from the rearview mirror. This was a car you notice, not one that blends into the scene, unless the scene is cruising in south LA.

She got into the behemoth and drove off in the direction of Salón Funtastique de Rodeo, in Beverly Hills. Jasón would still be there, closing up.

Angela put in her cell's Bluetooth.

"Call Jasón," she said.

After two rings, he picked up. "Angela!"

"Hey, Jasón. Are you free for dinner tonight? My treat?"

"Scrumptious! How about Yu/Mi Sushi?"

"Sounds good. I'll head over now."

"Fab, see you in about forty minutes?"

"Sure, I'll get there a little sooner, so I'll grab us a table."

"You got some juicy gossip for me?"

"Don't I always?"

"You're the best!"

Angela ended the call. She turned onto Santa Monica Boulevard. She was taking surface streets, as the freeway would be gridlocked at this time of day.

She found a parking spot right across the street from Yu/Mi Sushi long enough for the yacht. Amazing!

The place was packed, but there was a table for two in the far back. She ordered an iced green tea to drink while she waited for Jasón.

He quickly arrived, wearing a fashionably pre-torn white Gucci tee, white Bermudas and a white Levi's jeans jacket.

Angela stood up to give him a peck on the cheek.

"Love the Prada sneakers," Jasón said, after giving her a fashion scan. "Jealous! But what's with the all black, girl? Didn't you get the memo?"

"Cat burglar attire," she said.

"So, did you order yet?"

"No, just the tea. I thought we'd have a combo and sharezies."

"Perfecto!"

They ordered four types of sushi rolls, two of each, and some miso soup.

"So what's the scoop?" Jasón said. "Your job is so gruesome!"

"Well, this time you might actually be able to help me break the case."

"Oh, how exciting! Do tell!"

"Do you remember a client, probably some time last week. Blonde, tall, thin, gorgeous?"

"Honey, you've just described my entire client base!" He giggled.

"But you'd remember this young woman. Different. Pale, natural blonde, natural everything, green eyes. Probably not dressed to kill, and definitely not from around here. My guess is you had to talk her into a pedicure with your Funtastique Fuchsia."

"Oh, wait a minute. Yes! Unique creature. Slight accent. Not foreign, maybe Midwestern? Minnesota? Wisconsin? You know how they sound sort of Swedish, or something. She seemed really nervous. Not at home in her own skin. Oh, shit! She's not your latest Jane Doe is she?"

"Afraid so, my friend. The police have no clue, and until I see the death certificate I won't know how she died. Nothing obvious on the body."

"It really gets me how you can do that, look at all those dead bodies. That would so give me the willies."

"It's not pleasant, but it's my calling."

"You need a new calling, Angel!"

"Do you think you might have her name on file, or any contact info on her?"

"She's not a regular. I won't have much, and if I remember correctly, she paid cash, but I'll take a look."

Jasón pulled out his oversized iPhone in its hyper bling case.

"Now, keep in mind," he said, "I don't share client information as a rule, but as this one is not likely to sue me, I'll make an exception." He patted Angela's hand gently on the table.

After scrolling for a few seconds, he let out a high-pitched squeal.

A few heads turned briefly to look at them.

"I found her. Last Tuesday. Cassandra Michaelson. I did her myself. She was just such a dear. She asked me to call her Cassie. She said she'd moved here a few months ago for a job. Oh, crap, what was the job?"

"Take your time."

The miso soup arrived. Jasón dove in, exhibiting quite a flamboyant slurp.

"Wait!" He paused, spoon in mid-air. "Oops, gone again."

The suchi arrived and they both focused on eating.

"Excellent," Angela said. "Super hot wasabi!"

"Lovin' it!"

"Hey, did you go to your friend's gallery opening last Friday?" Angela asked. "How was that?"

"Hideous! I mean truly, truly sad. The paintings, so depressing. All black and red in those cliché violent brush strokes. The champagne was cheap and the cheese so very not French!"

"That's too bad."

"Ah! Got it! Cassie was an accountant. Talk about boring. She worked for some big financial firm downtown.

"That's strange," Angela said. "She didn't look old enough to be out of high school."

Some women were like that, Angela thought. They looked like they were twelve until they turned forty. Angela envied that, or did she? She suddenly remembered an article she'd read online yesterday about a major financial firm in Los Angeles facing charges of embezzlement. There were alleged organized crime connections involved. What was the name of that firm?

"Blyss & Hardingen!" Angela said.

"Blissed and hard again?" Jasón said, a little too loudly on purpose.

A few heads turned again. A peroxide-blonde man across the room sent a flirty wave to Jasón, who blew back a kiss in the air.

"No, Blyss & Hardingen, the name of the financial firm in the news," Angela explained. "Up on embezzlement charges, alleged Mafia connection."

"No idea what you're talking about. Well if she'd worked for them, I would definitely have remembered that name! I don't think she mentioned the name of the company, come to think of it, just that she was an accountant. Loved LA. Hated her new job."

"Well, if it was that financial firm, it would be a stupendous lead. Thanks, Jasón. You've been a huge help! Dessert?"

"No, I'm watching my weight. Did I tell you about the new love of my life, David?"

"I thought his name was Robert?"

"Oh, Robert is so pasé. David is yummy!"

"You are such the Casanova, my friend!"

"Proud of it!" Jasón flashed her his Hollywood-white grin.

Angela paid the check, left a large tip, kissed Jasón on both cheeks, and they were out the door.

She drove back to the mid-city morgue, taking the interstate this time, as traffic was moving again.

She parked Ernesto's lowrider a block from the morgue and walked to the same window she'd used to enter earlier.

She was about to change into her spiderwoman self when a large crow swooped down and landed on a tree branch near the window, chortling so loudly it made her jump.

"No haría eso si fuera tu," the crow said, in a gravelly voice.

"Whoa! You speak Spanish?"

"And *that* surprises you?"

"A bit, yes. So, what exactly wouldn't you do if you were me?"

"I wouldn't turn myself into a spider," he chortled. "I'm hungry. I might want a snack."

"What makes you think I was going to do something crazy like that?"

"Listen, I'm just trying to warn you that the mortician is still in his office."

"I don't see any lights on."

"His office is on the other side of the building. Go check it out, if you don't believe me. Better to wait until he leaves, no?"

Angela checked her cell phone. It was 8:47. She hoped the mortician wasn't working a night shift.

"Gracias," Angela said, giving the crow a suspicious perusal. Something about him seemed familiar, but she couldn't quite place it.

"De nada." The crow said and flew off.

That was sincerely weird, Angela thought. Was she turning into Doctor Doolittle now?

She walked around the rear of the building and indeed, there was light streaming from one of the windows.

She wanted to take a look in the mortician's office, so she'd have to wait until he left. She walked back to the car and sat inside. The fog was pulling in. It was getting chilly.

A little after nine, she saw headlights pull out from the morgue parking lot. The car turned in her direction. She leaned down onto the passenger seat, so as not to be seen by the mortician.

She waited a few more minutes, then pulled on her black gloves and black beanie. She walked to the morgue's window. No crow in sight. Spiderwoman time!

Once inside, she transformed back into her own body and turned on her cell's flashlight app. The ergonomics of shape shifting still baffled her. Where did her clothes, key fob, and cellphone go while she was a spider, and how did they rematerialize when she became human again? The Consortium never explained that very well. They just said it was the physics of metaphysics. Whatever that meant!

Angela found her way to the mortician's office. The door was closed but unlocked. Good, no need for spiderwoman. She went inside and swept the light from her cell phone over his desks. Neat piles of paperwork, pens in a metal cup. No clutter. There was only one file in his out box. The file tab read, "Jane Doe Case #3209."

Angela opened the file and right on top was the completed death certificate. Jackpot!

"Cassie," she whispered, "we're about to find out what did you in."

Angela scanned the certificate with her phone. It was just for the Consortium's private records. In the space for cause of death was typed: botox overdose. There was no indication on the certificate of this case being a suspected homicide.

The botox would explain Cassie's overtly youthful appearance, but she'd never heard of anyone dying of a botox overdose. Cassie didn't seem like someone who would have been getting botox injections. She was too natural, and seemed too innocent. Of course, LA was a brutal twenty-four seven beauty contest and could rope you into its addictive game in a flash, but Angela still suspected foul play.

There was certainly plenty of Botox in LA, and it was a neurotoxin derived from the same bacterium that caused botulism. It just seemed like a very expensive way to kill someone.

Then again, a lot less costly than losing a lawsuit due to the testimony of an expert witness. Maybe Cassie just knew too much. She'd certainly been in the wrong place at the wrong time. Welcome to LA! Now go home, in a box.

The other paperwork in the folder was a copy of the police report. Angela was tempted but didn't read it. Solving the case wasn't her job. She'd solved her part of the puzzle by finding Jane Doe's lost name. She closed the folder and on the cover, using one of the mortician's red-ink pens she wrote in large print.

"Legal name: Cassandra Michaelson. Occupation: accountant. Check to see if she worked for Blyss & Hardingen Financial. Possible homicide. She could have been an expert witness in the current embezzlement trial involving that company. Her death sounds like an organized crime solution to an unwanted witness problem! Oh, and, you're welcome."

She signed the note in cursive with a flourish, "Angel of the Lost & Found."

She placed the folder in the center of the desk, where the mortician would be sure to see it.

The police would handle the case going forward. She'd given them what they needed. They wouldn't ignore her note. A cold case didn't make the department look good, and this was not the first time the mortician had received an anonymous note from her. He'd know to trust it.

When she got back to the Cadillac, a crow was sitting on the roof. The same one who had talked to her earlier, she surmised.

"Hey!" She whisper-shouted. "Get off of there! Ernesto just washed and waxed this pink battleship!"

The crow hopped onto the driver-side rearview mirror, just inches from her.

"Successful venture?" the crow croaked.

"Yes, as a matter of fact." She looked the crow in the eyes. "Wait a minute, Ernesto?"

The crow chortled, then shifted into his handsome human form with a peal of laughter.

"Good one!" Angela said. "When did you take the shapeshifting course?"

"Last week. Aced it!"

"Congrats! Tough course. Thanks for having my back. That was sloppy of me, not checking for lights on the other side of the building. Might have been bad."

She doubted it would have been bad, just inconvenient, but he had come all the way here to protect her, so why minimize the risk factors.

"How did you even find me?"

"Had a gut feeling you might need my help." He slapped his firm abdomen. "Tracked your cell, headed for the nearest morgue in your direction."

"That's sort of depressing. Do I need to get a life?"

"Yes, you do! Hey, you know what they say about as the crow flies, well, it's true. No traffic. I just flew in from West Hollywood and boy are my arms tired!" He laughed at the stale stand-up joke.

"You flew here? No way!" Angela said.

"Way, but I'd rather not be flying around in the dark."

"You could change yourself into an owl. Great night vision. Or a bat! Even better. You can be Batman, I'll be Spiderwoman!"

"You are so loco!" Ernesto said, draping his arm around her shoulder. "I also came because I need my ride tonight."

"Sure, of course. Here are the keys, but you're dropping me home right?"

"Por supuesto, but I was thinking we'd grab a drink at La Descarga first. A little celebration? A little salsa?"

Angela had planned on having a quiet evening, a little TV, a lot of sleep. The salsa club was in the opposite direction from her place. She looked at Ernesto's handsome boyish face, flirtatious eyes, radiant smile. How could she resist?

"I'm not really dressed for dancing," she said, "but sure. ¡Vamos!"

Max

My name is Rose. I'm fourteen and taking some advanced courses at Galileo Academy for Science and Technology in San Francisco.

Five days ago, my life almost came to an abrupt end.

The last thing I remember was seeing Max. He's this cool homeless dude who sits on the bench in the park on the corner at Bay Street. He's super intelligent and has a warped sense of humor, just like mine. We say hello when I pass on the way home from school. Sometimes we talk for a while. He has soft jade eyes, a striking contrast to his mocha skin, and a bright smile that always makes my day.

I saw that smile turn itself off the instant the searing pain hit my lower back. Then I blacked out.

When I came to, my brain was full of a dense nauseating fog. I could feel a lot of pain in my body, but at a distance, muted. I was in a hospital bed, the kind with the metal bars on the sides. How did I get to the hospital?

Then I saw Max's smile again. What was he doing in the hospital? He was standing next to my bed, looking super concerned.

I must have passed out then, because the next thing I saw was my mom leaning over me, her face bigger than life. She was all blubbery with tears and her boozy breath made me feel sick.

I'm doing much better now, relatively speaking. I'm no longer in the Intensive Care Unit.

The doc told me I was lucky that the bullet missed my spine. It essentially passed right through me without doing damage to vital organs, but I lost a lot of blood and almost died. I've had restorative surgery and two transfusions.

I'm getting tired of being in this hospital bed. I guess that means I'm getting better.

They make me walk down the hall and back three times a day. It's no picnic, but I do it without complaining because I want to get out of here as soon as possible.

I could seriously do without the heavy doses of self-pity and angst from Mom and Dad's anger about this happening at all, as if I had anything to do with it.

It's Max who keeps me afloat like a Coast Guard regulation life preserver. He's here a lot, except when my parents are around.

Max fascinates me. Whenever I'd see him sitting on the park bench, he was always either looking at the view, which is awesome from there, or reading a book. Sometimes he'd be gone for a few days. I would miss seeing him then. We've been hanging out for about three months. I love our conversations. Last week, he was reading *Invisible Man.* I was reading it too. Not for school or anything, just because I wanted to. We talked about it. Here's a weird thing, though. We never introduced ourselves. We jumped right into more interesting topics and never got back to the basics. I started thinking of him as Max, though he doesn't know I call him that.

Max is no ordinary homeless dude. Maybe he isn't even homeless, just likes to hang out at the park. He does wear some pretty crappy clothes though, so I'm sticking with homeless. He's cool by me, whatever his story.

I've never told my parents about Max. They'd dump their judgmental crap all over him and tell me to stay away from him, like he's dangerous or something.

Max is sitting in the corner of my hospital room right now.

I move my head a little to the left so I can see him better. He's reading a newspaper.

"Can you come over?" I whisper.

Max moves the chair closer to the bed.

"Now, you just rest," he says. "The nurse'll come by and poke your arm some more soon enough."

"They don't want me to get any sleep," I complain. "Always taking something: blood, blood pressure, temperature."

"Ain't that the truth," he says.

His matted hair is tipped with a touch of silver which shines in the overhead light, making him look angelic.

"Max," I say, "do you know who shot me?"

I realize too late that I've said the name aloud for the first time.

"Max." He repeats, then smiles. "I like that name. Suits me."

"You were just in the wrong place at the wrong time." he says.

"So, it was like a random drive-by shooting?"

Sam just looks at me for a moment, but doesn't say anything.

I'm all spaced-out from the morphine drip, so I'm not thinking too clearly, but Max's brow is deeply furrowed and he looks like someone who has a secret he's not sharing. I stare at him. He must've been really good looking when he was younger. He's got a broad nose and high cheekbones. His skin is like milk chocolate, but with darker spots. Can African Americans have freckles? His eyes are a light green, like my dad's, except Max's are full of spirit. My dad's are all about calculation. Max is tall, muscular, and now that he's all cleaned up and wearing decent clothes, I can see he's really not that old, maybe closer to my dad's age.

"So what's your real name, Max?" I ask. "We never even introduced ourselves. How crazy is that, right?"

"They call me Samuel," he says quietly, looking down at his hands for a moment.

"So, do I call you Samuel or Sam?"

"Sam will do," he says.

The nurse comes in. She says I'm scheduled for another transfusion and she wants me to rest now. She gives Sam a stern look when she says that, as if he's the one who's keeping me from getting any sleep. I don't like this nurse much. She acts like I'm in here because I've done something bad, like it's a punishment or boot camp.

"I'll be going along then," Sam says. "I'll be back, soon as they let me," he smiles at the nurse, maybe teasing her a little. I can't tell if she likes it or not because she's already strapping the blood pressure cuff onto my arm.

Sam sits on the bench down the hall from Rose's room. He's thinking about the name she's given him. Max. It has a nice strength to it, a strength he doesn't feel he can own at the moment.

He thinks about Rose. That name oddly suits her, both the bloom and the thorn of it. He's been a regular presence in her life for a few months now. Long enough to see her change her natural blonde hair to a dark magenta and go from wearing a riot of color to wearing only black. Then came the nose ring and the rose tattoo on her arm, just a few weeks ago. Sam worries about her.

She's hanging out with him after school, instead of her classmates. She seems to be a loner, but these recent changes could mean she's trying to fit in with an edgy clique of other outsiders. He knows that scenario all too well. Teens with a disdain for all things mainstream and a desire to push limits, all limits. That could lead Rose into drug experimentation and criminal behavior. He spent the first two decades of his career in law enforcement as a parole officer for the juvenile detention system in Atlanta. He's seen the arc of this story line, and early in his own life, he lived it.

Sam wonders how this experience with street violence will affect her. Rose seems to trust him for the moment, at least to some degree. He's still a stranger, someone she can reach out to safely, without the strings and snares of familial relationships.

How will she react to the truth? It was a shock to him for sure. His head is still spinning. There is so much to consider. For now, the truth will remain his secret. She's got enough to deal with, and needs him too much, his presence, his rare blood type.

Rose's transfusion will take another hour. Sam takes a deep breath. Michael Ondaatje's novel, *The Color of Water*, rises up as it rests against his chest. The book is Sam's latest attempt to reach a deeper understanding of a conundrum that has, thus far, proven unfathomable. He's always been tortured by that inscription at the Temple of Apollo in Delphi, "Know thyself." How can you know yourself when your ancestral bloodlines trace back to unknown histories?

Still, in his case, it was his rare blood that brought him back into his own history.

"Hey, good afternoon, Sam."

Sam is pulled from his deep thoughts and looks up. It's Alex Mills, Rose's surgeon, and due to recent circumstances, Sam's confidant.

Alex smiles. "Got a minute to step into my office?"

"Of course."

Alex's office is amber from the late afternoon light filtering through slanted Venetian blinds.

"Have a seat," Alex says, as he sinks into his own leather executive chair behind a large oak desk covered with files and charts.

"We're lucky to have you, Sam, and I'm not just talking about your rare blood type. Do you think she suspects anything?"

"Now, what could she possibly suspect, Doc? That I'm a bored homeless man with nothing better to do than spend my day eating hospital Jello and flirting with the nurses?" He shakes his head. "She's got a lot to ruminate about in that brilliant head of hers, but she's always glad to see me. That much I can tell you."

"Can you tell me anything more about the shooting?"

"Only that the investigation will take time."

"I understand."

Sam knows more than he can divulge. He knows it was not a random drive-by shooting. An accurate shot from a fast moving vehicle is tricky and this perpetrator used a silencer. Sam's lead closed down a large meth operation a few days prior. He was definitely the target.

"I do have some big news," Sam says. "I quit the narcotics squad. There was an opening for a parole officer with the juvenile justice system here in San Francisco. I interviewed yesterday. With my level of experience, they hired me on the spot. I start as soon as the paperwork goes through, probably in two weeks."

"Hey, congratulations. That's great news. I mean, I respect the hell out of you for doing what you did, but it's time to step out of the line of fire, my friend. Any job that requires wearing a bulletproof vest seems like a bad idea to me."

"It's a miracle I had it on, Doc. I never wear it when I'm off duty, but one of those icy bay winds was blowing and my coat is pretty threadbare."

Well, you wouldn't be sitting *here* if you hadn't been wearing it while you were sitting *there*, believe me. That shot was aimed precisely at your heart."

"It packed a punch. I'll tell you that."

"Well, if Rose hadn't moved towards you as soon as you were hit, that second bullet would have killed her.

Sam knows it was intended to do exactly that. No witnesses. He unintentionally placed Rose in grave danger and can't forgive himself for it. His new position should keep him and her safe into the future.

Alex gets up. "Can I offer you some coffee? I'll warn you, it's been on the hotplate for hours."

"Thanks. I could use the caffeine."

Alex pours two cups. "Non-dairy is all I've got and I'm out of sugar.

"I'll take it black."

"Black," Alex repeats, combing his pale fingers through a tangle of short blonde hair. "Now that's the issue of the day isn't it?"

There is a brief silence between them.

Sam rubs his chin. "Does Rose's father know who donated the blood?"

"No, that information is protected by HIPAA."

"I had no idea he lived here, Doc. We grew up together, like brothers, until he started school. We haven't communicated in over twenty years now, not since I moved to Atlanta and took Mama with me. Once she was away from that house, she was so much happier. Still, she carried her secret all the way to the end of her life, God bless her. Afraid to speak the truth, even to me. Afraid of the repercussions, and for good reason. The South is still the South."

"I'm so sorry, Sam. So, how did you learn, if not from her?"

Sam chuckles. The laugh has a painful edge to it.

"There were plenty of rumors floating around when I was growing up, believe me. The truth is too powerful to be contained, but denial is a southern trait that runs deep. After Mama passed on, I moved west to get away from all the heaviness." Sam sighs. "Turns out, my past was right here, waiting for me."

"Life can be ironic, but also serendipitous, don't you think? I mean, San Francisco is not a small town. What are the chances that you would connect with Rose, after all these years?"

"Doctors believe in serendipity? You seem all science and facts."

"We see miracles all the time, Sam, things not explained by science and facts."

"Well, I sure do appreciate our talks this week. They've kept me sane. It's good to talk about these things. I rarely do."

"They were shared in confidence, Sam, and they will be kept that way."

"Thanks, and I apologize for being despondent."

"Didn't the nurses give you enough cookies and orange juice after your blood draws?"

Sam laughs. "Yes, they sure did, and I'm getting mighty tired of those vanilla wafers. Ain't you people ever heard of chocolate chip?"

"Talk to the budget office." Alex says. "I swear they get those wafers at one of those dollar stores." He takes a sip from his coffee and winces. "This coffee too, probably. It has a nasty bite."

"Bitter as they come," Sam agrees, "but don't knock the dollar stores. They've got some good eats in there, if you poke around a bit."

Alex gets up. "Let's go see how our Rose is doing."

They abandon their coffees and head down the hall.

After Alex and the nurse leave Rose's room, Sam pulls his chair up closer to her bed.

She smiles up at him.

"You know, watching the blood drip into my arm from that bag is really cosmic," she says. "It's not red, like you'd think it would be. It's maroon, like wine. It's like taking in a piece of someone else's life, of their soul even."

Sam smiles to see that the transfusion has given Rose some energy and cleared her brain a bit. She's more like herself again, a fountain of observations and insights.

"I have this rare blood type," Rose continues. "It's AB- like my grandfather's, but he died years ago, so they had to search for a donor. My dad has type A+ like my grandmother. Probably not too many people could be a donor for me."

"No. I'll bet not."

"I hear people with organ transplants start having memory flashes from the donor's life. That's pretty wicked. I was thinking this morning that it makes me less bummed out, you know, getting this other person's blood. It makes me feel like I'm not completely alone in here," she covers her heart with her hand. "You ever give blood, Sam?"

"Sure."

"Do you feel like a part of you is missing afterwards?"

"Never thought of it that way. It makes me feel useful, and the cookies is all right. Don't like vanilla wafers though, way too sweet. You like chocolate chip?"

"Who doesn't?"

"Well, when they let you outta here," he says, "let's go get us some freshly baked chocolate chip cookies."

"That's a deal. I'll even bake them myself."

"You know how to bake good cookies, Rose?"

"Nah, but it can't be that hard. My mom does it even when she's totally wasted." Rose frowns. "Guess that's not a nice thing to say about your own mother, but she is, you know, drunk a lot of the time."

"I'm sorry to hear that," Sam says. "Must be hard on you."

"Sad thing is, I'm sort of used to it."

Neither of them say anything for a while.

"Did your mom bake you cookies when you were a kid, Sam?"

"Oh, yes. Mama baked all kinds of things, corn bread, blueberry muffins. My favorite was her sweet potato pie." He bites his tongue. He should be more cautious.

"I could tell you were from the South. You still have some of the accent and the expressions. My dad's from Charleston, from one of those old Southern families. He loves sweet potato pie."

She gives Sam a shy smile.

"I'm not sure I should even tell you this. It's sort of embarrassing." Rose hesitates, but continues. "When my dad was a kid, they had servants and a cook, all African Americans. They were paid and everything, but still, kinda makes you cringe, right? He told me once that Miss Kora, that was the cook's name, used to make the best sweet potato pie. He and the cook's son would sneak slices out of the kitchen when she wasn't looking."

A touch of salt stings in Sam's eyes.

"You okay, Sam?" Rose asks.

Sam remembers the sweet, spicy taste of those stolen slices.

He wants to tell Rose that she has an uncle who loves her, that he is her uncle Sam, but he will wait.

Night of Falling Stars

The bouncer is snoring. His weight bears down on the rear legs of a wooden chair cocked precariously against the wall. His head is tipped back, jaw relaxed, mouth slightly open. His belly rises and falls in a slow rhythm, until someone jabs him with a pool cue.

The bouncer starts awake with a grunt, slamming his chair forward.

"Shit," he hisses, wiping drool from the corner of his mouth. "You suck, Al," he mumbles, then leans back to resume his nap.

The elk trophy above his head keeps watch through dust-covered eyeballs. It stares blankly at the opposite wall, where a blue electric waterfall advertising Olympia beer cascades perpetually down a rocky slope. The oval bar advertisement drones like a fish tank filter.

The young woman in the black cashmere sweater sits on a bar stool and stares at the waterfall too. It mesmerizes and disturbs her, like the pulsing glare of a TV in an otherwise darkened house.

She's never even heard of Olympia beer. Must be a local brand. Her straight, light brown hair is tied in a ponytail that cascades down her back almost to her waist. Even at twenty-seven, she looks more likely to climb a tree than worry about her makeup.

It's getting late, she thinks, only half listening to the booming voice of the heavy man who sits next to her. He's engaged in a monologue about trout. His eyes are glazed with alcohol and droplets of beer foam nestle in his beard and mustache.

The woman, a graduate student at MIT, has little interest in the art of fly-fishing.

She's tried to engage the fisherman in a conversation on other topics, engineering, physics, but they were not a successful match for Ed, originally from Darby, Montana.

In the past hour, she's acquired three glasses of beer, each from a different man in a plaid flannel shirt. All of them untouched.

Her name is Jana, and she's drinking a Manhattan. She'd prefer to be *in* Manhattan at the moment. Instead, she's in a roadhouse on Vashon Island in Washington State's Puget Sound.

Mitch, her older brother by two years, invited her to spend Labor Day weekend in Seattle. Last year, he landed his dream job designing video games for Nintendo in Redmond, Washington, a stone's throw from Seattle, and the self-titled Bicycle Capital of the Northwest. Mitch had always been a goof-off. Didn't do well in high school. She was valedictorian. He almost flunked out of college, she graduated top of her class. Now, he was making three figures a year to play video games. Mitch somehow always managed to be in the right place at the right time.

This time, it had been while running in the 1982 Boston Marathon. Mitch met and became best buds with the son of one of Nintendo's top execs. Go figure. Where was that kind of luck when she needed it?

Her own triumphs came only by hard work and perseverance. She believed in doing her best. Mitch believed in doing his best friend, or even his best friend's girlfriend. His success wasn't even remotely fair, but what else was new?

His success also hadn't matured him in the least. Jana was getting burned out on the chaos Mitch created by simply walking into a room, but he was her brother and she loved him.

Today, after a strolling lunch at Pike Place Market, he'd talked her into this excursion to Vashon Island.

The afternoon was enjoyable enough. They'd parked his new red Porsche 911 in the belly of the ferry at the Fauntleroy terminal, walked up to the observation deck at the stern of the ship, and watched the Seattle skyline grow slowly more distant. The weather was uncharacteristically warm and the sky was blue.

When they'd reached the island, Mitch drove way too fast on poorly paved roads to take them to his favorite beach. They walked along the rugged coastline, made sculptures out of driftwood, and laughed about childhood escapades. Then they had burgers at a greasy spoon diner. Mitch had promised a sunset return ferry trip, but hadn't realized that the ferries were running on a holiday schedule. They'd missed the last one.

So, Mitch drove them to this historic roadhouse. Then, after a couple of beers, he decided it would be terrific to go pick up a cycling friend of his who was living on the island. Since his Porsche only seats two, he'd left Jana at the bar.

That was over an hour ago. Mitch had promised to be back in a snap, but had neglected one thing: to grow up.

At first Jana felt annoyed and slightly bored. Now, she is angry. It's past eleven. The bartender is sober and seems like a nice guy. The bouncer is drunk and asleep. Jana can't imagine why this place even needs a bouncer.

It's hot and stuffy in the roadhouse, but she's nervous about going outside. The men are mostly old and busy playing pool. They seem as docile as Labrador retrievers, but you never know.

There is no point in calling a cab since there is no place else she can go, and she doubts there are cabs on the island. She'll just have to wait it out.

Ed, the trout fisherman, continues with his monologue.

"So, there I was thigh-deep in the Bitterroot River. It's raining hard, my waders are leaking, and I'm not catchin' anything but a cold. I'm about ready to call it a day. I reach in my pocket and pull out my knife and a hunk of salami. I slice off a piece. It tastes real good. Spicy. Picks up my mood a bit."

He laughs for no apparent reason.

"So," he continues, "I get to thinkin', what the hell, it's worth a shot. I hook a small chunk of the salami on the line and send it out. It's a perfect cast to midstream and I'll be damned if a second after it hits, I catch the biggest Rainbow! Shit, she was a beauty."

He snorts a laugh. His breath stinks of cigarettes, booze and a bad stomach.

"She must've been Italian," Jana says.

He chuckles.

"Did you ever try any other sausages? Pepperoni? Something German?"

"Heck, not a bad idea." He chuckles again.

All this talk about sausages is making Jana hungry.

"There wouldn't happen to be a place that delivers pizza out here, would there?" she asks the fisherman, without much hope of a positive response.

"Can't say that I know of any, but I bet we could weasel something out of Charlie. Hey, Charlie!" he calls to the bartender. "Ya got any pretzels?"

The bartender saunters over and puts a scratched up wooden bowl on the bar. He pulls out a jumbo bag of pretzel sticks and pours them out.

"Now Ed, don't you go wolfin' these down like you always do. Save some for, I'm sorry, we haven't had a chance to introduce ourselves. I'm Charlie, the proud proprietor of this classy establishment."

"Hi, I'm Jana."

"Good to meet you, Jana."

The bar phone rings. Jana wonders if it's Mitch.

"Excuse me," Charlie says and goes to answer. He talks briefly, then yells towards the small collection of overweight men at the pool table. "Hey Jake! Rita says she needs some help with Grandpa. He thinks it's World War II again."

"Aaah, crap!" the man named Jake says. "Tell her I'm on my way."

He slaps his pool pals on their backs, hangs up his cue, grabs a shabby parka off the coat rack, and heads for the door.

"See you fellas tomorrow," he says.

The jukebox chooses Bob Seger, who begins to croon "Down on Main Street" through overworked speakers.

Jana eats some pretzels. They're extra salty. She orders another Manhattan.

Charlie sets the drink gingerly on a fresh napkin. He reaches under the bar and pulls out the crossword puzzle from the Sunday *New York Times*. He offers it to her, along with a freshly sharpened pencil.

She gives him a quizzical look, surprised by the gesture and by the presence of the east coast newspaper here in the roadhouse.

He smiles and raises his shoulders in a conciliatory shrug.

"Thanks," she says.

"You're welcome. The Sunday crossword is the toughest you know. I can never manage to finish it." He lowers his voice. "Your friend's coming back, right?"

"He's my brother, actually, and I sure hope so!"

She starts in on the puzzle, although numbers not words are her forte.

She leans into the bar. *1 Across: Austrian-born Tony winner (1955).* Fat chance, she thinks, and moves on to the next clue.

1 Down: *traps.*

She stares at the puzzle. She can probably count the number of crosswords she's ever done on one hand, but it's something to distract her mind.

She takes a sip of her drink, bounces the eraser end of the pencil against the bar counter and focuses back on the clue.

Traps: a six-letter word beginning with an *S*.

"Traps. Traps." She whispers to herself.

"Once found a fox in an old trap," Ed comments. "Leg half torn off from struggling to get free. Nearly bled to death."

Jana gives Ed a sour expression. "Thanks for sharing."

"Had to put her down. Only moral thing to do." He clears his throat. "Still have the tail. Keep it in the garage."

Jana tries to ignore him. She's about to give up on 1 Down, and move on the next clue when the answer pops into her head.

S-N-A-R-E-S. She writes it in. Not bad for a science geek, she thinks.

She keeps working.

Ed offers suggestions whenever a clue relates to sports or geography.

Her sweater feels scratchy against the back of her neck and across her shoulders, where her skin is irritated from a mild sunburn, the result of all of that driftwood sculpture building on the beach.

She is searching for a nine-letter word for *standing ovations*, beginning with the letter *A*.

"Standing ovations. Standing ovations, starting with an A," she says aloud.

Charlie walks over, "Applause?"

"Nope," Jana says. "I need nine letters, that's only eight, but thanks!"

After a few more minutes of pencil tapping, she feels a gentle tap on her left shoulder, turns quickly, expecting Mitch and ready to slam him.

It's not Mitch.

It's a tall, strikingly handsome man, somewhere in his late thirties, she guesses. He's got brown eyes and long, raven black hair. He's clean-shaven and wears black jeans, a white, long-sleeved shirt, and a denim jacket. No flannel.

"Try accolades," he says, and flashes her a straight-toothed smile.

The word is a perfect fit.

"Mind if I join you?" The new arrival asks.

Ed leans over to Jana. "Better keep your eye on that one," he warns in a hushed, whiskey voice. "Likely hasn't seen a woman in months."

Charlie tries to hide a smile, and gives Mr. Tall, Dark and Handsome a knowing look.

Jana catches it, but is not sure of its meaning.

She nudges Ed gently with her elbow.

Ed winks at her and slinks away towards the pool table, chuckling softly.

She motions to the now empty bar stool on her right.

Her new crossword partner sits down.

She smiles, grateful for some fresh company. He smells a hell of a lot better than Ed, that's for sure, and might have something to talk about other than the virtues of hand-made flies over live bait. She has to admit, the salami story was pretty good, but she's not sure she believes it.

"You don't look like one of the regulars," she says.

"Then, that makes two of us."

"So, what's a nice girl like me doing in a joint like this? No offense, Charlie."

"None taken," Charlie says, then wanders off to the other end of the bar to deliver two beers.

"Well, let me guess." Her new crossword partner gives her some serious perusal. "You're a sociologist doing a study on the courtship behaviors of Northwestern lumberjacks and fishermen."

"Not bad, but nope. Try again."

"Okay."

He rubs his chin and raises his eyebrows in mock consternation.

"You've inherited a ramshackle estate and you're checking out the social scene to see if you want to sell the place pronto or have the kitchen remodeled."

"And you," she says, pointing the pencil's eraser accusingly at him, "must be in advertising."

"Ha! Well, if you call spending ten years writing copy for a hardware catalogue being in advertising."

He gives her a sheepish grin. "Actually," he whispers, "I'm a novelist, but don't let that get around. They might not let me play darts here anymore."

"Our secret," she promises.

She takes another sip of her drink. "So, have I heard of you? You know, New York Times Best Seller list, that kind of thing."

He rolls his eyes. "I doubt it. My agent hasn't even heard of me!" He laughs. "Sorry. It's rude to laugh at your own jokes."

"Nah, just means you don't get out enough."

"Now that's the truth."

He gives her another perusal with some dramatic flare, "So, let me see. Third time's the charm, right?"

"So they say."

"You came here with some hot shot in a red Porsche, but he left hours ago and you're wondering if you should shoot him when he returns, if he returns."

"Hey, how'd ya know?"

"Oh, these old guys have good ears and they like to talk."

Charlie wanders back over. "What'll you have, Behr?" he asks.

"You're welcome to one of these," Jana says, pointing to the three beers. "On second thought," she adds, "I'm sure they're flat and warm."

"Thanks," Behr says, "but no thanks! What I need is coffee."

"Black with lots of sugar," Charlie says.

"So, you *are* a regular." She teases.

"Can I get you another of whatever you have there?" Behr asks.

"No, no thanks. I've hit my limit. Gone past it, actually." She smiles. "I'm Jana. Bear, now that's an impressive name. What's the story? Did you kill one bare-handed?"

She suddenly wonders if he's Native American, and she's just put her very white foot in her very white mouth.

"You're right on both counts, though I've never killed a bear with or without gloves. It's an old German name for bear, but also an old Dutch name meaning naked. B-E-H-R. So take your pick, or maybe go with naked bear."

"I like that. Very rugged, though I've never seen a bear with clothing, except Paddington Bear, of course."

Behr smiles, "Of course."

Jana wonders if the conversation is getting awkward. She's relieved when Behr starts telling her about his first novel, a murder mystery set in the rail yards of Seattle. His second was a sequel to the first. Both had only marginal success.

Charlie sets the coffee on the bar with a kind smile for Behr. Jana notices the affection.

She tells Behr about life in Boston. She's in a challenging graduate program in chemical engineering. She has a complex relationship with her parents. Her dad is a civil engineer and her mom is a retired tennis pro. Her Peter Pan older brother, Mitch is why she's stranded in the bar. She talks about the East Coast, how it feels cramped and imploded compared to this place.

He talks about growing up just north of Seattle. Both of his parents were high school teachers. He has his three older sisters, all beautiful, all brilliant. His third novel, the one he's currently writing, is a psychological thriller about a would-be shaman whose ambitions take him further into the underworld than he'd planned.

Their conversation is comfortable.

"Hey, the juke has gone silent," Behr says. "An opportunity for us! Any requests?"

"I'll take some Motown, if it's in the mix."

"You bet."

He heads for the old jukebox.

Jana wonders if Mitch has driven his Porsche into a ditch, or over a cliff, and if she should be worried. She decides to forget about him for now. He's obviously not thinking about her. Sleepiness is edging in on her thoughts. She's not a late night person.

Behr, on the other hand, must be. Who goes to a bar at almost midnight to drink coffee? Maybe he wants to work on his novel when he gets back home.

Behr returns looking triumphant as "Heard it Through the Grapevine" starts up.

"Excellent choice!" Jana says.

She's grateful for the break from the previous mix of country music and heartland rock.

After three more Motown hits, Mitch shows up, his arm around the waist of a small blonde woman and a grin on his boyish, freckled face.

"Jana! Looks like you did okay!" he says, nodding his head in Behr's direction. No apologies forthcoming.

Jana frowns. She should have seen it coming that the cycling friend would be female. That explained why Mitch was gone so long, and perhaps it even explained why he wanted to take an excursion to Vashon Island.

The cycling friend, Laurie, has the face of a prom queen and the body of a cheerleader. Her eyes are dilated. She looks seriously stoned.

Jana would really like to give Mitch one where it counts, but she's actually glad he isn't dead. Hanging out with Behr has mellowed her mood. She'll save her rant for tomorrow.

"Hi ya, Behr!" Laurie says, adding a nervous giggle.

"How are you, Laurie?" Behr returns.

There's a moment of awkward silence between them all, while Aretha Franklin belts out, "R-E-S-P-E-C-T."

"I'm so sorry we kept you waiting all this time," Laurie says to Jana. "It's really not Mitch's fault. I couldn't get my roomie's kid to go to sleep."

Mitch suggests they drive back over to Laurie's place to hang out on the back patio. There's a huge meteor shower going on.

The bar must be closing soon, and Jana's not sure where she and Mitch will be able to sleep for the night. Maybe Laurie will be a blessing in retrospect, if she has some extra beds at her place.

"So, are you up for a meteor watch?" Laurie asks Behr.

"Well, as much as I love astronomical events," he says, "I think I'm going to pass."

Laurie pouts, "You see, it's just that Mitch's car only seats two people."

"Oh, sure. No problem," Behr says. "Where's your place? I'd be happy to drop you off there."

"Cool. Rd. 149."

"Okay, then." Mitch says. "Groovy!"

Charlie gives Behr a gentle hand on the shoulder and says, "I'm open until 2:00."

Jana thanks Charlie for being such a great host and waves goodbye to Ed, who's playing pool.

She gathers her coat and purse. They all head out to the parking lot.

"Nice truck, Behr." Mitch says. "Did you do the restoration yourself?"

He and Behr launch into a manly discussion about Behr's immaculate, forest-green 1957 Chevy.

It's damp and chilly outside. Jana pokes Mitch in the arm and herds him towards his Porsche. Laurie is already sitting inside, long legs crossed. She's got the interior light on. She's applying a fresh layer of firehouse red to her lips, staring into the vanity mirror on the back of the visor with rapt attention.

So much for riding with Mitch, Jana thinks. She's too tired to fight about it and hopes she won't regret that later.

"Don't drive too fast, Mitch!" she pleads. "We won't be able to keep up."

She gets into Behr's truck, scooting onto the wide bench seat. The vinyl feels cold through her jeans.

They twist and bump over the dirt roads of the island's interior, following the Porsche's tail lights.

The roads are narrow and dark. They are numbered not named. Rd. 127, Rd. 128. Tall pines line the shoulders like silent giants.

Jana thinks about Behr. She really knows very little about him, just his first name. Where he grew up. That he obviously loves his three older sisters. That he's thinking about moving back to Seattle. That his first and second novels had some marginal success. He's a bit mysterious. There's a darkness behind his eyes.

They rumble past miles of forest. The world is a labyrinth of moonlit evergreens and the sky is a narrow, twisting ribbon of star-spangled black furled overhead.

Jana places her hand on the dash to steady herself.

Mitch abruptly turns into a gravel driveway on the left. Behr's truck is less graceful. It breaks and turns with a rugged jerk and comes to a lurching halt.

"Whooo!" Behr says. "Your brother is crazy!"

"No kidding!" Jana says, stretching to release the built up tension across her shoulder blades.

Mitch and Laurie get out of the Porsche and walk over to the truck.

Behr rolls down the window. The air outside smells of pine and wet earth.

"Go on and walk around the house," Laurie says, motioning with a long, slender arm. "I'm going to grab a few blankets."

"Hmm," Behr says. He turns to Jana. "Do you want me to stay a while? I mean, I hadn't planned on it, but it looks like the situation here may be a bit awkward for you if I leave."

"Any situation involving my brother is awkward for me," Jana says. "It's super late, but if you wouldn't mind sticking around for a little while, I'd be grateful. You did say you liked astronomical events."

"This would be the Perseid Meteor Shower," he says, "and yes, I'd be happy to watch for a while."

They all end up on a large deck behind the house and recline onto some funky old chaise lounges, the kind with the vinyl straps. The stars are a riot of brightness. They look like they've gotten a wash in a jewelry-cleaning machine.

Laurie comes out from the house and hands everyone a wool blanket.

Jana pulls a slightly moth-eaten Pendleton up close around her chin. Mitch and Laurie are somehow huddled together on a single lawn chair; their bodies make a squirming lump under an unzipped sleeping bag. Laurie's nervous laughter escapes in muffled bursts.

Jana and Behr sit reclined in two separate lawn chairs.

After long minutes, they still haven't seen a single meteor.

"There!" Behr says, pointing into the star-crammed sky.

"Missed it," Jana says, still looking hard, disappointed.

After about thirty-minutes of stargazing, the wind picks up and high clouds move in.

Jana and Behr saw sixteen meteors between them. Mitch and Laurie weren't really looking.

They all go inside to warm up.

"My roomie's gone for the weekend," Laurie chirps.

Mitch grabs her and starts to nibble her ear. More giggles.

"So stay the night," Laurie says, more like a command than an offer. "You can sleep in there." she says to Jana, pointing down the hall to an open bedroom door.

Then Laurie and Mitch disappear into another bedroom and close its door behind them.

"I'm too tired to think straight," Jana says, mostly to herself. She looks at her watch. It's 1:55 a.m.

"I really need to sleep," she says.

"I hear ya," Behr says. I'll head out. Thanks for your company. I've really enjoyed it!"

"I've enjoyed it too," Jana says, sorry to see him leave.

She suddenly feels a little fearful of being in this stranger's house. She knows it's silly, stupid really. She's stayed in tons of hotel rooms alone during conferences, but this house is in the middle of nowhere, surrounded by dense forest.

It's a dark, dark, dark place. As a small child she was deathly afraid of the dark.

As Behr walks away she hears herself say, "You could stay." Then, realizing she may need to clarify that, adds, "I mean this looks like a pretty decent couch."

Then, she thinks that seems rude. She doesn't want to be rude, and stumbles on, "I mean, what I mean is..."

Behr turns to face her. "It's okay. No worries. I'm not keen on driving home, and I'm fine with crashing on the couch."

"You are really something," Jana says.

"Hey, I grew up with three sisters, remember. I'm good at slumber parties."

"Good night," she says, grateful to have him in the house. They give each other a brief hug.

Jana goes down the hall and enters the bedroom at the end. It's large and cluttered. She steps around piles of clothes on the floor. An overstuffed closet stands open. A bra and negligee hang from the edge of a large vanity mirror.

She straightens out the unmade bed and decides to sleep on top of the comforter and under the Pendleton. She keeps on clothes. She rolls up her down coat for a pillow.

It's cold in the room. She keeps on the small lamp by the bed, and lies down on her back staring at the web of cracked paint on the ceiling.

She tries to sleep. The light is keeping her awake. She reluctantly turns it off.

The comforter smells like stale perfume, something flowery. She drifts in and out of scraps of dreams. Eventually, she drops into a dreamless sleep.

She is jarred awake by a loud, male scream from beyond her closed door. It's not Mitch. It must be Behr.

"Holy shit!" she says, sitting up, disoriented.

She reaches for the bedside lamp, knocks something on the floor. She finds the lamp cord and flips the switch.

The light startles her. She sits still and waits, not sure what to do. It's quiet again.

She gets up, pulls on her boots and heads for the living room. Behr has been a godsend to her, she wants to make sure he's okay.

She finds him sitting up on the futon couch, the wool blanket draped over his legs. He's still fully dressed like her.

He looks ghostly, distant. He's combing his fingers through his thick, black hair. His breathing is uneven and he is shaking.

A jolt of adrenaline races through Jana's sleep-laden blood. Maybe this isn't a safe situation. Maybe he isn't stable. He sure seemed stable earlier, but he could secretly be a psychotic axe murderer for all she knows. He writes murder mysteries!

She turns on the side table lamp by the couch.

"Behr," she whispers, not getting too close to him. "It's okay, I'm here."

If things took a bad turn and she screamed, would Mitch even come and protect her? He and Laurie have already ignored Behr's scream, and it was loud.

Behr sighs deeply. He seems to be coming out of some kind of stupor.

"Are you all right?" she asks, half ready to bolt.

He clears his throat. "I'm sorry," he says. I'm really, really sorry. I must've scared the crap out of you."

There's a long silence.

He continues in a whispered voice.

"I still get these nightmares sometimes. It's been sixteen years." He takes in a deep breath and blows it out, clears his throat again. "Vietnam."

He says the word as if it explains everything. Maybe it does.

Gray, pre-dawn light is coming in through the window. Behr's image reflects in the mirror across the room. He looks like a large animal has mauled his soul.

"Jesus," Jana says. "You wanna talk about it?" She's not so sure she wants to hear whatever he may have to say.

"I'm sorry," he says again, turning to her.

She sits on the couch next to him and reaches her hand out to him, a reflex of compassion. He takes it and holds it against his chest. She feels distant, numb. To her, this suddenly seems like a Hungarian film with Russian subtitles.

"Mommy?" a small, scared voice asks from out of the dark.

It's so unexpected, Jana stifles a scream.

A blonde boy, maybe three years old, waddles over to them.

"Your mommy's not here right now, honey," Jana says, in as soothing a tone as she can muster. Her voice sounds gravelly. "Do you want a drink of water?" The question is well intentioned, but sounds idiotic.

"Where's my mommy?" the child asks, with bewildered curiosity.

Laurie's sleepy voice down the hall calls, "Joshua?"

The child turns and runs down the hallway.

"That was creepy," Jana says. "Why do they have horror movies with demon children in them? We shouldn't have to be afraid of children, I mean really!"

Her heart is still racing.

She and Behr sit silently for a moment.

Jana wonders what kind of person leaves her small child in the care of an irresponsible roommate for the weekend. Her mind fills with questions. What kind of a person leaves his younger sister in a bar full of lumberjacks on a wooded island in the middle of nowhere for hours? What kind of person hops into the cab of a vintage Chevy truck belonging to a tall, dark and handsome stranger, and allows herself to be driven away through the dense trees to end up in the bed of the kind of person who leaves her small child with an irresponsible housemate? She feels tears welling up.

"Now you look like *you* could use some support," Behr says, then laughs softly, breaking the tension.

Behr seems back to his previously solid self. He puts his arm around her shoulder and they both lean back and rest their heads on the back of the couch.

In the pre-dawn light, Jana watches a thin-legged spider move over the ceiling above them, its long, spindly legs testing every step in its gravity-defying journey.

Your choices can spin a web that ensnares you. It can happen so quickly, that you don't even realize it is happening. She knows this.

The woman whose little boy just came into the room probably knows this all too well.

Behr must know it too.

Jana leans into his shoulder. "I hope you won't find this too forward a question, but I'm just wondering. You and Charlie, are you two, you know, together?"

"You are very observant. We were lovers several years ago. Now we're just friends, well, more like brothers really. We help each other stay sane, whole."

"I thought there was some chemistry."

"Well, you are the chemist, so you'd know."

She chuckles. "I just noticed the compassion, the small gestures of affection. Those are rare between men, at least between the men I know. Then there's my brother who is pretty much clueless."

"He's a piece of work."

"And he's not likely to do the work it will take to change that. He's almost thirty. I think I'm done waiting for him to grow up. I used to really look up to him because he was my older brother."

"Well, older doesn't always mean wisdom."

"No kidding! I'm done putting up with his crap. I'm definitely done with being the victim of it. I had some hope that this move to a new environment, away from his immature friends, would give him a chance to break his patterns, but it looks like he's just transferred them right onto his new life."

"That's got to be hard on you."

"Yeah, well it sucks for him too. He's just too busy having fun to recognize it yet, but it'll catch up with him."

"I think you're probably right."

"But we were talking about you, before I got off track. Does your family know? Are they supportive of your choice?"

"I'm lucky. My parents are liberal old hippies, and my sisters just treat me like one of the girls. They just sent me this terrific shirt."

"I thought it looked rather haute couture for this woodsy place."

"Yeah, I should probably opt for something more LL Bean, but weirdly Vashon is pretty hip. Maybe because it's an island and people tend to ignore each other's idiosyncrasies in order to keep the peace."

"You're not going to tell me Ed knows, are you?"

"Ed got transplanted here a few years ago and now he's wedded to the place by virtue of his Nisqually wife. He's a character for sure, and a goodhearted old fart, but no, he just thinks I'm an eccentric hermit."

"Well, I'm making a pact with myself, and you're my witness. This will be the last time I visit Mitch. I don't want to get caught up in his chaotic lifestyle anymore."

"Sounds like a wise plan."

"I mean, just because you love someone, just because they're family, doesn't mean you should put up with their obnoxious behavior. If he never changes, then that's his loss."

"He was a real jerk last night."

"I know, right?"

"Well, I don't suppose we're going to get any more sleep. The sun's about up. Shall I go see if Laurie has anything decent to eat. I make a mean omelette."

"Sounds good to me."

An owl hoots loudly somewhere outside, a last call in the passing night.

"We're going to need some strong coffee!" Jana says, getting up.

Behr gets up too. They give each other a long hug.

"What a night!" Jana says. "Maybe you should give Charlie a call, let him know you're okay."

"I used the phone in the kitchen and called him last night, since he was sort of expecting I might return to the bar. I assume he is sleeping soundly right now."

"And so is Mitch, of course! Why do narcissists always get a better night's rest?"

Behr looks out the window at the dawning light. "Yeah, but they miss the catharsis of sunrise."

El Regalo (The Gift)

Jill stepped into *El Mercado de San Juan,* a huge indoor market in Mexico City. The massive warehouse space buzzed from the activity of hundreds of vendors selling their wares at stalls piled high with colorful fruits, vegetables, exotic foods and spices. *Piñatas*, dresses, handbags, dolls and ponchos swayed gently from wires above the narrow aisles, caught in the cross drafts.

Wandering through the market, Jill tried to understand the rapid-fire Spanish bombarding her brain from every direction. It was impossible, so she allowed the experience to flow over her. The melding of so many voices sounded like an aviary of tropical birds, all calling for her attention.

After twenty minutes, her red mesh shopping bag with the traditional image of Our Lady of Guadalupe was still empty. She didn't need anything, she was leaving in the morning, but wanted to buy something. She got a pumpkin empanada for her breakfast tomorrow, a cheese tamale for dinner tonight, and a mango for a snack. Her limited Spanish got her through the transactions at three different stalls. She meandered towards the exit, gratified to have experienced this slice of authentic Mexico City life.

Near the exit, she noticed a small stand selling herbs and teas. The male vendor, who looked to be in his nineties, smiled at her. His teeth were remarkably healthy and white. He gestured with his hand for her to come see his wares. In Spanish, Jill asked if he had hibiscus tea. The hostel served it chilled and sweetened, a Mexico City favorite called *Agua de Jamaica.* She could give the tea to the hostel hosts as a small thank you.

The old man nodded, said something in Spanish so quickly that it might as well have been Arabic. Jill didn't understand a word. He showed her a large bag of the tea. Jill nodded, asked for the price, paid him and said, "*Muchas gracias.*" It wasn't much money. Then the old man said something else in Spanish, looking Jill directly in the eyes with great attention. She recognized only five words: *regalo, especial, niña, su,* and *abuela.* Gift, special, girl, her, and grandmother.

Well, he'd gotten the gift part right. She wondered who the girl and the grandmother might be, perhaps he was talking about his own family. His face reminded her of the men she'd seen in the Aztec history murals by Diego Rivera at *El Palacio Nacional* the day before. The high cheek bones. The long, elegant nose. The fierce look of the eyes.

The vendor went to the back of the stall, then returned with the tea wrapped in some old newspaper. He handed the package to Jill. She smiled and thanked him again. People in Mexico City were extra polite. She put the bundle into her shopping bag and headed back to the hostel.

When she unwrapped the old newspaper, she found not only the tea, but also a small model car, a pink Cadillac convertible. The rear left taillight was missing, so was the passenger side rearview mirror. The paint was a little scratched and faded. *Regalo, especial, niña,* and *su abuela.* A special gift for a girl and her grandmother? Who was the girl? Was she the girl? She was twenty-four, hardly a child, though to someone approaching the century mark, less than a quarter of a century might seem child-like. In any case, she had no time to go back and ask. The market closed at sunset. It was already dark.

She'd take the toy Cadillac home as a serendipitous gift. Her only travel bag was already stuffed with other treasures, two shawls embroidered with colorful flowers. One with a blue background for her mom, one in red for her Grandma June. For her brother, Donald, she'd bought a t-shirt depicting the Mayan calendar. She'd also gotten a pair of leather *huaraches* for herself. She wrapped the Cadillac back into a single sheet of newspaper and tucked it inside of one of the sandals. She was ready for her flight to San Diego.

Back at her tiny cottage in Ocean Beach, just two blocks from Sunset Cliffs, Jill put the pink Cadillac on the bookshelf in the living room. It looked happy there, between the blue basket of seashells and the brass mermaid statue.

In the face of her day to day reality, Mexico already seemed like a dream.

Work was hectic, as usual. Being an Operating Room Tech in the ER was exhausting. Weekends were all about sleep, something she didn't get enough of during the week. Lately, she looked forward to that sleep even more than usual because of a strange recurring dream.

In the dream, she sat in the passenger seat of a pink Cadillac Seville convertible, the real car after which the toy one was modeled. The driver's seat was always empty, yet the car sped through the desert along a highway with no other traffic, under a sky streaked with brilliant stars.

When she awoke from these dreams, she felt refreshed and rested. Something she hadn't felt since she started the ER job almost two years ago.

The dreams came only on the weekends and felt like a special gift. She wished they would come during the week too, when she needed them most. She moved the toy pink Cadillac to her nightstand, hoping that might encourage the dream to show up more frequently.

It did. The dream became a nightly experience. After a week, Jill was no longer in the passenger seat. She sat behind the wheel. She felt the leather steering wheel cover against the palms of her hands, the wind in her hair, the ball of her foot pressing down on the accelerator. No matter how hard she pressed, however, she couldn't change the car's speed. She also couldn't turn the steering wheel. The car was not under her control.

Every night, Jill tried to make the Cadillac slow down so she could pull to the side of the highway. After four nights, she could make the car go more slowly, but still was not able to turn the wheel and pull over.

That Saturday night, she easily pulled the car off the road and stopped. She opened the door and got out. She walked cautiously among the ancient Joshua Trees in the moonlight. The crisp air cooled her face.

The Joshua Trees, a species of tall yucca plants, looked so real. She reached out to touch a long spike and immediately felt a painful jab on the tip of her index finger. The spike had drawn blood.

Suddenly, she was awake. She sat up in bed, turned on the bedside lamp and looked at her finger. It was bleeding.

She got up. In the bathroom, she put some antibiotic gel and a bandage on the small wound.

She took a deep breath. Her heart was racing. The dream had always made her feel so relaxed. This was not a positive development.

Had she been sleepwalking in the cottage and gotten her finger poked by something sharp? She doubted that. Maybe she was astral traveling. She'd heard about that phenomenon. It was an out-of-body experience in which the soul travels on its own.

But her soul didn't prick its finger on the Joshua spike, her body did. So, what was going on?

She picked up the pink Cadillac cautiously, still spooked. She went into the living room, switched on the light and put the car back on the book shelf. She was tempted to go outside and toss it in the garbage can, but that seemed too harsh.

She noticed a book title on the shelf directly below the Cadillac. "The Teachings of Don Juan: A Yaqui Way of Knowledge," by Carlos Castaneda. Her brother gave it to her a few years ago. She enjoyed the read, but doubted any of it was true. Castaneda apprenticed with a Yaqui medicine man named Don Juan, who led him through a series of paranormal experiences. These were induced by ingesting peyote, the flower button of the mescal cacti that grows in the deserts of northern Mexico and contains a psychotropic substance. Peyote is usually ingested as a tea. Jill had no interest in taking peyote, but maybe she would read the book again. It might offer insights into the dream experience.

After all, the pink Cadillac came from *El Mercado de San Juan.* San Juan, Don Juan. The musical theme from *The Twilight Zone* came to her mind, and what about that old vendor who gave her the toy car? He might be a medicine man. He sold all kinds of dried herbs and teas. The intense look he gave her still haunted her memory. Who knows, maybe his name was even Juan, a common enough name in Mexico. She laughed at the thought.

On Sunday morning, Jill decided to go for a walk up on the cliffs and to the beach. She hadn't done that in months. The weather was perfect, sunny and mild. She put on shorts, a tank top, her new sandals, a baseball cap, and was out the door.

Jill loved going to the tide pools. Watching the small creatures move around and the purple sea anemones open and close with the rush of water was soothing. Their lives were so simple. She wished her life could be more like that. Simple.

Up on the cliffs, the majestic beauty of the Pacific Ocean spread to the horizon, with waves crashing on the rocks into plumes of white foam. The cliffs were about twenty feet wide, with more narrow stretches, where the sandstone had further eroded. Eventually, the cliffs and the expensive homes built at their edge, would collapse into the sea.

There were always old men in dirty clothes gathered on the cliffs to talk, smoke, fish and dream of better days, past and future. Troubled teens with tattoos, body piercings, and torn black clothes hung out there too. They glared menacingly at the sunburned tourists in their clean white Bermuda shorts passing by, holding their small children safely by the hand.

Jill loved the cliffs for their unfiltered juxtaposition of nature's grandeur with society's vulnerable underbelly.

She and Donald, who was a few years older, used to come here on Sundays with peanut butter and jelly sandwiches, plus a cooler of juice boxes. They'd hand them out to anyone who was hungry or thirsty. The old men never turned them down. The troubled teens were takers as well. Once they dropped their tough exteriors, they were just kids, laughing at sick jokes and getting stoked by a particularly tall wave plume, just like everyone else.

Jill couldn't even remember the last time they'd had a PB&J Buffet, as they called it. Working at the ER had hardened her, made her grow a bitter edge around her heart. She missed her old self. Optimistic about humanity. Her acts of adolescent kindness were perhaps naive, but also authentic.

When she got to the long stretch of Ocean Beach beyond the pier, it was crowded with co-eds from the various colleges and universities in San Diego. Everyone was getting in a few more days of beach time before school started up again.

Jill grew up here, making sand castles as a kid. Boogie boarding all through her adolescent and teen years. No time or energy for that these days. She wasn't even tanned anymore. The ocean had fallen out of her routine, which had become all work and no play. What did they say about that? It made Jack a dull boy? Well, it made Jill a dull gull. She laughed. That was two laughs in one day.

Jill walked a few blocks up Newport, OB's main drag, with its tourist shops, juice bars and tattoo parlors. Then she cut through the narrow streets of the town, using shortcuts through alleyways.

Back home, on her futon sofa, she felt her sun-warmed muscles relax and a smile travel all the way to her soul.

She'd planned to keep the pink Cadillac in the living room for a while. The last dream was too disturbing, but the eternal rhythmic pulse of the ocean had mellowed her. She put the car back on her nightstand, wanting to see what happened next.

That night, she was driving the Cadillac somewhere in the Mojave desert, under a new moon. The Milky Way stretched across the sky like a magic carpet of diamonds. She drove for a long while in the peaceful desert night. Then, way up in the distance, she saw a lit billboard. When she reached it, she pulled off the road and looked up. The billboard was painted black. It had a question written in large white letters.

"Does this path have a heart?"

The white letters pulsated, like little beating hearts. Then they lifted from the black background, floated up into the sky. Flying around, they each turned into white doves. Then, the doves shot up into the cosmos, becoming stars.

Jill woke up to the beeping of her alarm clock. It was 4:00 a.m. Another manic Monday. Time to go help the ER doctors save some lives. Too often, their job entailed patching up knife wounds, extracting bullets, and setting another broken bone on another broken human being who had chosen to abide on the wrong side of the law.

"Does this path have a heart?" Jill asked herself, thinking of her job. It had seemed like it when she'd first started out, but now, she wasn't sure.

On Tuesday, she took the Castaneda book to work to read during her lunch break.

Jill was surprised when she ran across a familiar sentence. "Does this path have a heart?" The sentence on the billboard was a direct quote from Don Juan! She felt a chill run up her back. She closed the book and put it into her purse. The nurses were coming out for a smoke. Time to vacate the picnic table.

Jill read a few chapters every day at lunch, then finished the book on Saturday. She called her brother. She hadn't seen him since before her trip to Mexico.

"Hey, Donaldo!"

"Jilligan! What's up?"

"Watcha doin' tomorrow? Wanna come over and help me do a PB&J Buffet out on the cliffs?"

"Wow! That's a blast from the past. Yeah, cool. I'm totally there."

"Okay. Great."

"I'll swing by the store on my way over and pick up everything we need."

"Sweet!"

"What time do you want me to be there?"

"Ten? We can catch up while we spread the peanut butter and jelly."

"Spread the love, Baby!"

"You crack me up."

Donald arrived right on time, wearing a Hawaiian shirt with surfboards on it, and a pair of clashing striped board shorts.

"You are such a dude!" Jill said, taking one of the shopping bags from his arms. It was heavy. She put the juice boxes into the fridge.

"Organic apple," Jill read aloud from the package. "Juice boxes have evolved since we were kids."

"I know, right?"

"We can sit at the dinette set. There's not enough counter space in the kitchen. Want some coffee? I brewed your favorite. Kona."

"You bet!"

"Oh, I have something for you. I bought it at a museum store in Mexico. Thought you'd like it."

She got the t-shirt, wrapped up in some blue tissue paper, and gave the gift to him.

"You're the best, Sis!"

He took off the wrapping and held up the t-shirt.

"A Mayan calendar! Super cool! Thanks!" He gave her a hug.

They organized their supplies and got to work.

"So when does school start up?" Jill asked.

"Week after next, but I have some teacher prep stuff this week."

"Still lovin' it?"

"Totally. The kids are a challenge, but I manage to get some math into their brains, through the thick fog of hormones. What about you? The ER. That's one tough job."

"Yeah, it is."

"But you love it?"

"No. I think I'm done with working at hospitals. It's not my path with heart."

"Hey, have you been reading, "The Teachings of Don Juan?" Donald asked.

"Yeah. Thanks for giving me that. It's eye opening."

"So, any idea what your path with heart might be?"

"That's the problem. I'm stumped."

"I'm sure you'll find it. Knowing that the path you're on isn't the one for you is the first step, right?"

"Yeah, I guess so."

They made and wrapped sandwiches in silence for a while.

"Okay. We are good to go," Donald said. "Hey, let's bodysurf afterwards."

"Okay. Sure. I'll bring a suit and get us towels."

Out on the cliffs, they sat on the cement wall on folded towels and offered their free buffet.

There were no takers for a while. People had gotten more wary. Eventually, some of Donald's old-timers, who knew him and trusted him, showed up. They were happy to munch, sip and tell their stories. Donald used to come down to the cliffs often when he still lived in OB. He'd let the old guys use his cellphone to make medical appointments or other needed calls.

Once the PB&J Buffet had proven itself benign, some of the teens in their black clothes came over and joined in. After an hour, the sandwiches and drinks were all consumed.

The beach was always crowded on weekends, but Sundays were a bit more mellow than Saturdays.

Jill felt the thrill of the waves as she tried to stay in their powerful push as long as possible. The ocean always woke up her spirit.

Afterwards, they watched surfers ride under the pier and back out. A lifeguard hopped on a rescue jet ski nearby, heading into the surf. A swimmer had gotten too far beyond the breakers and was being pulled out to sea by a rip current. OB had a lot of those. You had to be alert.

"What about being a beach lifeguard?" Donald asked. "I mean you were born and raised here. No one knows this stretch of ocean like you do. You swim like a fish, you're strong, and you'd be helping people, saving lives even."

"Is that even a career choice?" Jill asked. "I thought it was just something college students did in the summer for minimum wage."

"Maybe, but I'm sure there are pros involved. You should check it out. You could help get people to the ER, if needed, without having to deal with what happens to them once they get there."

"Your brain is so quirky."

He was right, though. She loved being near the ocean and helping people. She already had all of the emergency medical training, plus a ton of experience in crisis situations.

"I'll look into it," she said, though still skeptical that it could be a real career.

They headed back to the cottage. Donald didn't stay longer. He needed to go home to get ready for a dinner date with his girlfriend.

Jill ate a simple meal, and went to bed early.

She tapped the Cadillac on the nightstand. "Let's go for a drive," she whispered."

She turned off the light and went to sleep almost immediately.

Back in the Cadillac, she drove on I-5 heading north up the coast, with no traffic, the interstate felt eerie.

The stars above her disappeared as a light marine layer pulled in from the ocean.

She had no idea where she was going, but as this was always the case in the dreams, it didn't matter. She hoped that tonight she'd discover something that would help her find her path with a heart.

Suddenly, an old man sat in the passenger seat next to her.

It shocked her so much, she almost crashed into the center guard rail.

Could she crash in the dream? A scary thought.

"¡Ve al apartamento de tu abuela, rápido!" the man said, gesturing with his hands as if conducting an orchestra. He looked like the vendor from *El Mercado de San Juan*. She swore it was him.

"Go to your grandmother's apartment, quickly," he repeated, in English this time.

Her Grandma June lived in Carlsbad, about twenty miles further north.

With no other traffic or cops, the speed limit was irrelevant. The Cadillac easily cruised at 90 mph. It felt exhilarating to drive that fast.

How would she get inside of grandma's apartment? She didn't have a key.

"No te preocupes por eso," the man said, reading her thoughts. She decided to call him Juan.

"Okay, I won't worry about it."

As soon as she reached the apartment parking lot, Juan disappeared, as mysteriously as he had appeared.

She opened the apartment's front door. Maybe doors were never locked in dreams.

She found her grandmother in bed, in severe distress. Jill knew the signs. Grandma June was in cardiac arrest.

Jill grabbed the phone on the nightstand and dialed 911. She got the dispatcher and explained the situation. She took her grandmother's hand and talked softly to her, trying to keep her as calm as possible. Soon, she heard the siren of an approaching ambulance.

She woke up in her own bed to the sound of her cellphone ringtone. The caller ID said it was her mom.

Why was her mom calling in the middle of the night?

"Mom?"

"Jill. I'm sorry to wake you up, but Grandma June had a heart attack. She's in the hospital. I'm there now. The doctors say she'll be okay. The paramedics got to her in time."

"Oh my God!" Jill said, both at the news and at the realization that it was a dream come true, with a very bad twist on that phrase.

"Can you come? It's Tri-City Medical Center in Carlsbad. The same place we used to visit Grandpa."

"Of course," Jill said, still trying to wrap her head around what just happened. "I'll be there as soon as I can. Is Donald there?"

"I'm calling him next. Jill," her mom hesitated for a moment. "Grandma June's conscious, but a little loopy. She says you called 911 for her, and then held her hand while waiting for the paramedics to arrive. She kept calling you, Angel Jill. Is that sweet, or what?"

A special gift for the girl and her grandmother, Jill thought.

Had the vendor at the market in Mexico given her the toy Cadillac so she could ultimately save Grandma June's life? That was more than a special gift. It was *un milagro,* a miracle.

It seemed impossible. Maybe Grandma June had been able to reach for the phone and dial 911 herself, but then why had she seen an angel who looked like her own granddaughter? Jill's head was spinning.

She'd call work from the hospital in Carlsbad and say she wasn't coming in, due to a family medical emergency.

It would take her forty minutes to reach Carlsbad, driving up the coast in her truck at the speed limit. She grabbed the toy Cadillac and put it into her purse, just for luck.

A path with a heart, she kept thinking, as she drove up I-5. She saved her grandmother's heart in the dream, maybe in real life too. If the yucca spear could prick her finger and make it bleed, then she might actually have made that 911 call in her grandmother's apartment and held her hand. Not just in the dream, in real life. That was indeed *un milagro*, but it was also more than a little creepy.

Just before the exit she needed to take to get to the medical center, she saw a brightly-lit billboard on the right. It had a red background and white letters. The message blew her away.

"Save lives! Become a California State Park Lifeguard. A job with heart! Training starts in September."

Were dream messages coming into her waking life now, or was that billboard for real?

It hadn't occurred to her that since the lifeguards worked for state beaches, they worked for the California State Park System. That changed the scenario for her, made being a beach lifeguard a career option. A surge of joy ran through her. This felt like her path with a heart!

"Thank you, Juan!" she shouted, "and you too, Don Juan!"

Now that her grandmother was safely in good hands and a path with heart lay ahead of her, would the pink Cadillac dreams continue, Jana wondered. She hoped so!

From the South
and Further South

The World's Largest Ball of Bras

Kyle Semack is working his summer job at Fink's. He's stocking canned pork and beans when the pink Cadillac pulls up and parks across Main in front of Dot's Diner. Kyle is listening to *Black Sabbath* on his Walkman and wouldn't have noticed a thing if it hadn't been for the clap of thunder just then, loud enough to be heard even through the heavy metal din in his ears. He looks up for a moment and just about glues his nose ring to the grimy glass when he sees the behemoth payload on the flatbed trailer behind the Cady. It looks to be at least thirty feet in diameter.

He pulls off the headphones.

"Hey, Jodie! Come on out here!" he shouts to his younger sister, who is back in the bakery frosting cupcakes for the weekly St. Augustine charity dinner.

"Cain't!" Jodie shouts back, in her squeaky voice. "Got ma hands full."

"Damn it, Jode. Y'all gonna miss it. Ain't never seen nothin' like it. Shit."

Kyle walks right on out of the store without even removing his *Fink's Friendly Helper* apron.

It's nearly noon and mid-August. The rains haven't set in, and Ida, Louisiana, a stone's throw from Texas or Arkansas (take your pick) is a good place to fry okra on the sidewalk.

Kyle scuffs up to the thing in his black work boots. There's every sort of bra in that ball, and there are layers of them, so you can see them not just on the surface but down behind each other. There are fancy ones, plain ones, lacy ones, black ones, light yellows, hot pinks, ones with flowers on them. He even sees one with little Tweety Birds, and a few of those athletic kind. Then there's one, right on the surface, makes him wish he could meet its previous owner.

That big ball of bras is creating it's own sort of gravity, pulling Kyle in like a planet of female mystery. That kid is just about in a trance, ready to reach up and touch a lacy red one, when he notices a heavyset man in a light-blue leisure suit stepping out of the diner. The man is wearing a ten-gallon without a spot of dust on it. Kyle figures he must belong to the pink Cady.

"Well, howdy!" the man says, walking up to Kyle with a used car salesman's smile pasted on his fat shiny face.

He extends a large hand. "Name's Bill, Big Bill Barns. Out from Lubbock."

As they shake, Jodie comes walking across the street towards them.

"Whoa!" she says when she gets close, turning red and putting her hand up to shield her eyes from the sun.

"Let me give y'all the grand tour," says Big Bill. They walk around the trailer to the back, where a spot of shade hangs on them from the only tree on Main.

A large sign on the trailer's bumper boasts: "World's Largest Ball of Bras."

"No shit!" Kyle says, pushing a long strand of violet-streaked hair out of his eyes. "How many would ya say are in there?"

"Don't know as anyone's actually kept a count," says Big Bill. "Twenty thousand, maybe more."

"How long y'all been doing this?" Jodie asks.

Jodie is wondering how high that ball would bounce if you dropped it out of an airplane. She reaches, bewitched, to touch a cup of blue satin. It feels cool against her finger, like moonlight.

Kyle is quietly repeating over a rap beat in his head, Big Bill Barn's Big Ball o' Bras. Big Bill Barn's Big Ball o' Bras. Big Bill Barn's Big-Assed Ball. He laughs, letting the air puff loudly through his closed lips.

"You're soooo rude!" his sister hisses.

Big Bill seems oblivious.

"Well, I didn't actually create the thing, you see," he explains. "I'm just its most recent proprietor. Acquired it after a stunt in Arizona. "Bras Across the Grand Canyon," is what they called it.

"You mean they stretched 'em all the way across?" Jodie says, her eyes looking like they are about to pop out of her chubby, still pimple-free face.

"All the way," says Big Bill. "Though, regrettably, I did not witness the event myself."

Big Bill chuckles, imagining the sight, his belly shaking under the blue suit.

Dude must be burnin' up in all that polyester, Kyle is thinking, as he stares lustfully at a white lace number with little pink roses right where the nipples would be. "You could train a whole damn football team on this thing," he says. "Snap! Snap! Snap!"

Jodie kicks her tennis-shoed foot against the thick rubber sole of Kyle's boot and scowls.

"So," Kyle says to Big Bill. "After they stretched 'em 'cross the canyon, they rolled 'em up into this here ball and sold it to you?"

Kyle starts to thinking about his girlfriend's black lace one, the one that unhooks from the front.

"That's 'bout right," Big Bill says.

"Must've cost a fortune," Jodie says. "Now what'cha gonna do with it?"

"Oh, gonna see how much bigger I can get 'er. Travelin' some. Taking more donations. Maybe get me one of them Guinness World Records."

"You mean this ain't no world record yet?" Kyle says.

"Oh, I reckon it is, but ain't no harm in adding a few more. You care to make a donation today, young lady?" he says to Jodie. She flushes and looks about ready to crawl under the nearest rock.

Dude, can't you see she ain't got nothin' yet, Kyle is thinking.

"Got me a donations bucket right here." Big Bill continues, encouragingly, leading them around to the other side of the ball.

Kyle can see a few good-sized items inside the white plastic bucket, and can think of a couple of young ladies at the high school who might have an item or two of interest to add to Big Bill's Eighth Wonder of the Modern World.

And then, there's Mrs. Big Bill to consider. She walks out of the diner in a low-cut summer dress the color of bubblegum. She has bleached hair, sapphire eyes, and a smile that would sell a lemon that don't even run, right off the lot for a good price. She can't be more than half Big Bill's age.

Woo-wee, Kyle is thinking, her bra could reach across that canyon all on its own.

"This here's the Mrs.," says Big Bill with pride. "May June, these here young 'ens are takin' a mighty interest in our investment."

He pulls a crisp white hanky from his pocket, lifts off the Stetson for a moment, and wipes the sweat from his face and balding head.

"We 'bout ready to roll, Doll?" he asks the Mrs.

Jodie blurts out, loudly and to everyone's surprise.

"Y'all don't gotta leave right away do ya?"

A few other folks are braving the heat to come see the ball up close and personal. Carver Jones and three of his clients from the barbershop, Al Sterling, Ray Lobinsky and Artie Gonzales, virtually hop across Main like eager rabbits. Emily and Claire Ann, the waitresses at the diner, giggle in front of the window and egg each other on to go outside.

Within minutes, there's a small crowd and Big Bill and the Mrs. are happily giving tours.

Macy Sue from the Sears catalogue store struts down the sidewalk twirling her dainty pink donation. Kyle can't help staring at the shape of her breasts bobbing gently under her blouse, and he's feeling pretty grateful about having left on that thick, green grocery apron.

Jodie is staring even harder than Kyle, wondering what Macy Sue looks like without any clothes on, and lamenting that she herself will never look anything like that.

Macy Sue drops the bra into the bucket and receives a round of applause and lots of whooping from the men.

"Wow!" Jodie says, under her breath. "This is soooo cool."

"Yeah," Kyle agrees, then realizes it's his baby sister he's talking to.

"Come on, Jode," he insists. "We best be headin' on back."

"Are you kiddin'?" Jodie says, flushed with excitement.

"No. I don't think you ought be watchin' this."

"Who're *you* ta tell *me* what to do!" Jodie screams. "Who do you think you *are*, anyway? Just 'cause Daddy's done gone, don't mean I gotta listen to *you*!"

Kyle throws his sister an *I'm gonna kill you* look.

Everyone else is nonplussed by her outburst. Jodie Semack is everyone's sweetheart, a quiet, gentle child, not yet twelve.

Luckily, Macy Sue comes over and hugs Jodie's red-haired head to her chest, making all the men envious.

"Sweetie," she says in that molasses voice of hers, "Y'all just come along and we'll get ourselves a cool root bear float or somethin' else nice." She and Jodie head towards the diner.

Jodie turns and gives that ball one last longing gaze.

Kyle stares at his sister's flushed face in the glaring sun, wanting to hate her, but realizing instead, and much to his dismay, that she might just be pretty one day.

The Trouble with Hal

Charlene DuBois waited in the checkout line at the Winn Dixie. Her silver compact reflected a pink-lipped frown as she scrutinized her ash blonde hair. The humidity was bringing out the curls she'd worked so hard to control since her teens. That was eons ago.

She was no innocent child anymore. Not that she had been all that innocent, even then.

Still, she had always done the right thing. Dated the right boys. Gone to the right schools. Married the right man, though that was a matter of opinion, namely her father's. She'd raised four healthy Christian children, a long line of thoroughbred horses, and trophy winning Standard Poodles. She had always been a good girl, until now.

So, here she was at sixty, a former homecoming queen, still attractive in a tight-fitting white linen suit, still everyone's sweetheart and the perfect southern belle.

If only they knew what was in her trunk at this very moment, it would be the scandal of the decade, and it had been a juicy decade.

She closed her compact with a snap, dropped it into her white leather bag and began piling her groceries and the dozen boxes of baking soda onto the conveyor. The young cashier's dark hair was pulled back, revealing her pale neck. She had a lovely complexion, but her dark eye shadow was all wrong.

"Have you ever thought of going to a lighter eye shadow, dear?" Charlene asked. "Let me give you my card." She rummaged through her purse. "I have some new colors that would be stunning on you."

"Excuse me?" the girl said, in that way teenagers have, like they own the world and what are you thinking even being on the same planet with them.

Charlene decided to skip the card, it was clear it would be wasted on this child.

She signed the credit slip with her usual flourish and wheeled the squeaky cart outside.

The hot air blasted her face with the smell of exhaust fumes from a diesel delivery truck driving past. She hurried back to the car, searching for the keys in her purse. Sweat was forming on her upper lip as she pushed the cart up to the pale pink Cadillac Allante. She'd received the car as a bonus for topping the sales charts at Mary Kay.

She thumbed the button on the electronic key, releasing the trunk. It was a habit. The smell was overwhelming. She quickly slammed the trunk closed. Looking to make sure no-one had seen anything. The parking lot was almost empty.

What was the matter with her? She was getting sloppy. The stress was getting to her. She opened the left side passenger door and lifted a paper bag from the cart, it was over-stuffed. She was having a hot flash, as if it wasn't hot enough already. A pack of English muffins flopped out and landed at her feet. She put the grocery bag on the back seat, then bent down to retrieve the muffins. Her head was spinning.

It had been three days and she still hadn't figured out what to do about Hal.

She really needed to do something, and soon. The smell was starting to get into the passenger compartment. She'd noticed it on the way out to Crawfordville, the nearest decent grocery store. Now she had to drive back the twenty-minutes to Panacea in the worsening stench.

She wished she could use Hal's truck for needed errands, but that was too risky. She had parked it behind the barn, out of sight. She'd deal with it later.

She was beginning to regret not informing the authorities. It was too late now. She'd made her decision and was stuck with it. Unfortunately, she was also stuck with Hal in the trunk.

She hadn't killed him. It was an accident, but she had no way of proving that.

What if some of the more troublesome women in town decided to throw suspicion on her? There was no *way* she'd let Hal's misfortune land her in prison in her golden years! He had already stolen decades of her life. His emotional abandonment, narcissistic behavior and philandering would not be missed.

She'd planned to drop his body in the marsh out by Hungry Point. It would take months before anyone found him, if they found him at all. There were gators in that water.

The night she drove out to the marsh was surreal, something from a movie or a sleazy detective novel. She took the old gravel road just past the golf course, driving without headlights for the ten slow miles to the edge of the swamp at two in the morning. The moon was a thin crescent and the gravel grinding under the tires occasionally hit the bottom of the car, sounding like random gunshots. Her nerves were a shambles before she even reached the water.

Charlene didn't know how in mercy she'd gotten Hal onto the plastic tarp in the trunk in the first place. It was a blur. Maybe it was the big punch of adrenalin that hit her bloodstream right after Hal's glutinous appetite did him in. Getting Hal back *out* was another matter.

She'd recently seen a show on how the ancient Egyptians lifted eighty-ton stones to build the pyramids using only wooden levers, but she was no Egyptian. Even with rope and a shovel for leverage, she could hardly budge the body. She weighed only 110 pounds. Hal weighed well over 200, and that was when he was alive and holding his own. The Cadillac trunk was too deep and she was, after all, just a tiny grandmother.

She struggled for twenty minutes. Every time she got Hal a little closer to freedom, he'd rolled right back into the trunk again. All she got was spooked and exhausted. She gave up and drove home again.

So, there he was, her unfaithful Hal in his silk Armani pajamas, surrounded by twelve opened boxes of Arm & Hammer and decaying all too quickly. She'd get those fresh boxes in there right away, not that it would help much. The situation was out of control.

Still, there were the long-term benefits to consider. No more muddy golf shoes on her Persian carpets. No more slurped coffee and lip smacking at breakfast. No more gaudy gold chains on his overly-tanned chest. No more of his flirting with waitresses and sleeping with God only knows whom, maybe even that pale faced, makeup moron at the grocery store. No more hours of real crime TV shows, though some of those *had* proved useful. Most importantly, no more sleazy embezzlement schemes and gambling debts that sucked away at their retirement savings. She was better off, no doubt, but stuck with a big package of circumstantial evidence.

Package. That was it! A new plan occurred to her. What she needed was her Dad's old freezer, the big one in his garage out back. Her father had been an avid hunter and game fisherman up until the stroke three years ago.

The smell was getting worse.

She turned the air conditioner on high, dug into her purse for her atomizer and gave the air several shots of Mary Kay Live Fearlessly Eau de Parfum.

She got onto US-98. The traffic was oddly heavy. She heard the siren of a police car approaching and her heart raced until it thankfully moved past her. Then the traffic came to a dead stop. She jabbed the button to open the window and get some fresh air, even if it was hotter than Hades, and turned down the visor to check her face. It needed adjustment. She took out her lipstick. It goes to figure, she thought, that Hal would be as much trouble dead as he had been alive. She had wanted to be rid of him for years, and now that she was finally freed from his presence, he was *still* tagging along like a ball and chain.

A big man in a Ford F150 in the next lane was making kissy faces at her.

"If you only knew, Sweetheart," she said to herself, giving him her freshly applied, Parisian Rose smile, but her smile was wearing thin.

Maybe she made a huge mistake by not calling 911 immediately when Hal started having trouble from her exceptionally hot jambalaya. That might have saved him. She gave him some antacid and thought that was all he needed. When he dropped dead on the kitchen floor, the intense rush of adrenaline in her system made her panic. The hyped-up courtroom drama they just watched after dinner didn't help matters. She freaked out about the potential repercussions of his death. What if she were accused of poisoning him? That led to a severe anxiety attack that ended up with Hal in the trunk, and her in some deep doo-doo.

In the light of day, why would anyone accuse her of poisoning him? She'd eaten the jambalaya too, and without any negative results. She had as many character witnesses as she would ever need to vouch for her moral integrity. She was a pillar of the community, the Chair of the Wakulla County Garden Club.

Still, there were always those women who smiled to your face but relished creating havoc behind your back. To them, you were just competition and taking you down was their greatest pleasure. The nastier the tactics, the juicier the spoils, as far as they were concerned. She hadn't wanted to take the risk. Ah, well. What was done was done.

The traffic was starting to move again. When she got to her exit, she took off, leaving pickup Joe to kissy-face at her upside-down bumper sticker, "Blonde and Proud."

She turned into the driveway of her ranch house and parked the car in the detached garage. She opened the tops of all the new baking soda boxes and lined them up on the dryer. She wheeled the trash container next to the trunk, tied a handkerchief over her nose and mouth, took a deep breath, held it, opened the trunk, yanked the old baking soda boxes out, tossing them in the trash. She closed the trunk, took a few deep breaths, held the last one, and opened the trunk again. She quickly placed the new boxes around Hal's body, sprinkled some baking soda over him for good measure and slammed the trunk closed.

She went into the kitchen, washed her hands thoroughly, put away the groceries, fed the dogs, checked for phone messages. Everyone thought Hal was out of town on business, meaning he was off somewhere playing Poker and betting on anything that could run or fight. He wasn't due back until the day after tomorrow. She'd tell everyone he simply hadn't come home, had probably run off with some floozy. No one would raise an eyebrow at that. All the folks at the First Baptist knew he was a two-timer. Some of them knew from personal experience, she strongly suspected.

She took a quick shower, changed into dark pants and a red shirt, tossed the keys to her father's house in her purse and headed back to the car. It was 2:30, her father would be napping for hours. She drove the five miles to his place below the speed limit, although she wanted to floor it.

She unlocked his kitchen door and reached in to grab the garage key from its peg. She needed a roll of butcher paper. It was heavy and hard to move, but she managed to drag it to the car and get it into the back seat. She took several packets of white deli labels and put them in her hip pocket. She found the electric carver in the tool drawer next to the freezer and put it on the floor by the passenger seat. She took a magic marker from the glove box and went back to the garage.

She opened the top of the freezer, a puff of condensation cooling her face. She counted the packets of frozen meat and fish. They all had serious freezer burn and were quite inedible. That was the beauty of it. Venison/1-1998. Elk/3-1998. Merlin/3-1998. She made a new label for each of the forty-three packets, making the letters and numbers look like her father's shaky cursive, easy enough since her own hands were trembling. It took way too much time, but it had to be done. When she was finished, her hands felt so frozen, she could barely cap the pen. She closed the freezer and rubbed her hands together. All she wanted was to wash her hands of this entire mess, but the mess was just getting started.

She was pretty sure her father had a wet-dry shop vac. She poked around. Everything was covered in cobwebs and dust. She must look like a complete wreck, she thought, and it was only going to get worse. She could see an orange extension cord hanging from a nail, she took it, just in case hers didn't reach far enough.

"Oh, what a tangled web we weave," she sighed, pulling a strand of sticky spider web from her hair.

This job wasn't going to be easy, but she was resolved. She might look dainty, but she wasn't squeamish. She was born and raised on a horse farm in central Kentucky and had birthed many a foal. She was still an avid horsewoman with four Arabians in the stables. Shoveling shit was nothing new to her, but she'd need a mighty big shovel to clean up this debacle.

She spotted the round, red shape of the shop vac tucked in behind the gardening tools, half obscured by Old Glory. She shook the dust out of the flag, folded it with reverence and placed it on the workbench, then rolled the vac to the car and heaved it clumsily into the passenger seat.

She was exhausted already and she had a long night ahead of her.

She walked around to the driver's side, pausing for a moment at the rear bumper. "Just a few more hours, Hal," she whispered, tapping the trunk, "and your Houdini act will be complete."

She locked the garage, returned the key to its peg in the kitchen, locked up the house and got back into the car. It was so oppressively hot, she opened all the windows. Her hair was already past saving.

She drove along Midway Road. The radio started playing, "Stand by your Man." She quickly turned it off, and made left onto Happy Trails.

Happy Trails. Of course! Why hadn't she thought of it before? She could back the car up to the end of the gravel drive by the stables. She could saddle up her steadiest Arabian, Big Mystique, tie ropes to the four grommets on the tarp and then tie them to the pummel horn on the saddle. Big Mystique would provide the muscle she lacked.

She would do the work on the gravel, where she could hose everything down afterwards with a mix of water and bleach. She'd empty her dad's freezer of the stale packets of meat and fish, replace them with the newly wrapped packets, then take the old ones to the county landfill. Done.

As she turned the corner onto Gambado, she could see her ranch house down the road. Her eldest son's silver minivan was sitting in the driveway. Her grandchildren, Jeremy and Alicia, were running around in the front yard, blonde hair flying.

She pulled to an abrupt stop at the side of the road under a weeping willow. She took a quick inventory of the loaded car, especially the red shop vac leaning dangerously to starboard.

She tugged her rain gear out from under the passenger seat and tossed it over the vacuum. She turned down the visor and sculpted some order into her ravaged hair, extracting a few lingering cobwebs. She freshened her face and hands with some wet wipes from the glove box. A touch more lipstick, a quick dab of powder and she looked half decent.

She drove toward her house. The children spotted her car and started jumping and waving. No sign of their parents as yet, a mercy.

She hit the automatic garage door opener, maneuvered past the minivan in the driveway and pulled inside the detached garage. She hit the button again to close the garage door. She got out of the car, took a deep breath, slapped the dust off of her slacks and hurried through the garage's side door, locking it behind her.

"Who wants lemonade?" she shouted cheerfully, as she sauntered across the lawn, arms outstretched to greet her approaching grandchildren.

Summer Serenade

Beulah heard it while resting her tired old lady bones in the red Adirondack chair. It was a sound out of kilter with the heat and the fading light filtering through the magnolia tree. Bagpipes.

At first, she thought it was a fancy car horn, but the melody kept changing and at the end of each short phrase, the tone slumped as all of the air expelled from the bags. Then there was a long pause, as if the piper were waiting for courage to mount anew.

Not one to miss an adventurous moment, Beulah pumped herself out of the wooden chair, grabbed her straw hat from the side table and headed out of the yard.

As luck would have it, the pipes stopped altogether as soon as she'd left the garden. She waddled down the full length of the back alley, but all was quiet. She wished the piper would play again, so she could ascertain his location.

She ambled towards the public park along Maple, stopping briefly to chat with Nora Lanthrop, who was still recovering from her episode. Nora insisted she had known a woman in the Old Country who'd played the pipes every morning at five.

"Not a stitch of clothing on her, just standing right out in the middle of the street," Nora said.

Beulah was never sure what to make of Millie's stories, though she was certain they were no more than half true.

Beulah found nothing of interest at the park, just some boys tossing a baseball. No piper. Then one of those dreadful leaf blowers began making an awful racket, sending her scurrying towards home, hands over her ears.

She arrived home tired and grumpy, but nothing a touch of sweet iced tea with fresh lemon wouldn't cure. It had been an adventure indeed, but she had not found the highlander and his bag of tricks.

Her iced tea resting on the side table, Beulah settled back into the Adirondack. Her son, Carlton, had bought the old chair at a garage sale on the coast. It needed a new coat of paint, so Beulah's grandson Darren had painted it firehouse red at her request. Sitting in the chair, she liked to pretend she was driving a convertible Maserati in the Tuscan countryside. Her children no longer allowed her to drive, claiming her eyesight was too poor. She'd put up a good fight, but in the end, had lost the battle on that one.

No sooner had a merciful sigh escaped her thin, tea-whetted lips but those pesky pipes were at it again. Beulah recognized the tune this time, lilting itself into the sunset sky.

"Oh, Danny boy, the pipes the pipes are calling," she sang along, softly.

Now, wasn't that enough to char your waffles, she thought. The pipes are calling all right, but nobody's there when you answer!

She wasn't about to go play hide and seek with that piper a second time.

The melody changed. It seemed louder and closer than ever, but maybe that was just the fading light making everything more available to the ear.

Beulah shook her head, then sang along in a warbling soprano, a little off key.

"You take the high road and I'll take the low road."

As night fell, the piper stopped blowing and Beulah went reluctantly into the house.

She slept poorly, those Scottish airs kept showing up in her mind like commercials for laundry detergent. Her bed was lumpy and her life too near its winter to endure such summer smoldering.

In the morning, she went on her weekly shopping trip to the Piggly Wiggly with Charmaine, the assistant who came every Tuesday, even though Beulah didn't need any help. She'd only agreed to let Charmaine come along because Laura was stubborn and insisted she should have a companion when she went out. Nonsense, but Charmaine was a nice enough girl, if a bit slow on the uptake.

Beulah finished her afternoon supper. The air in the house was hot and stuffy, so she headed for the Adirondack in the shade. She rather hoped to hear the highlander again, but what were the odds he'd return? Perhaps she had only imagined him.

In her chair, Beulah was about to nod off when the drone of the pipes startled her wide awake. They sounded as if they were in her very yard. She sat upright in the chair, slid her legs to the side and got up with a slight groan. She walked to the edge of the yard and peeked through the tangle of honeysuckle on the fence. Nothing to see but the neighbor's ornamental plum. It seemed each direction she tried, the pipes were floating in from another. She found herself circling, tilting her head from side to side.

She circumambulated the Adirondack three times before she was willing to believe her ears. The sound was undeniably coming from the chair itself! When she walked away from it, the volume noticeably decreased. When she walked towards it, the volume increased. She got down on all fours and checked the grass beneath the chair. Maybe one of her grandchildren had put some smarty-pants electrical doohickey that played music down there. All she got for her foraging was eye contact with a pill bug, dirty knees and palms and a moment of panic when she wasn't sure she could recover a dignified standing position on her own. Luckily she could, but the process was far less than dignified.

She was worn plumb out. She went into the house, washed her hands and splashed some cool water on her face from the faucet in the downstairs restroom. She could hear nothing but the slow drip of the faucet, which her son had promised to fix two months ago. She looked at her old lady face in the mirror, adjusted her hair and decided that she was going bats and needed a vacation, or some sort of medication, or at the very least a strong mint julep.

She headed back out into the now darkening yard and found the chair to be perfectly quiet. The flowering magnolias perfumed the air with their slightly sour sweetness. She touched an armrest hesitantly. Solid and silent. She took her hat which was still on the side table and went back into the house, determined to call the doctor in the morning.

Beulah slept remarkably well. The morning dawned cloudy and the air was heavy with the promise of summer thunder. She was relieved. No need to sit out in the yard if it were raining, and no need to bother with calling the doctor.

She would take the bus to Greensboro and visit her old friend Luann. No one would need to know. It would be her secret excursion. She'd mention her pipe dream, so-to-speak, and see what explanation her friend might have.

Luann was a little eccentric but smart as a whip, and she made a lovely mint julep.

Alas, Luann was completely out of bourbon and, of all things, insisted that Beulah had a haunted chair. Luann went on and on about some television show she'd seen that claimed antique furniture could be haunted by the ghosts of previous owners. Some of these ghosts, according to Luann's account, were far more of a nuisance than Beulah's highlander, so she ought to be grateful, in that respect.

Here Beulah had gone all the way to Greensboro for some sane advice, only to receive an ear full of hearsay one might read in one of those tabloids they sell at the Piggly Wiggly check-out counter. Woman gives birth to twin chimpanzees, or some such hooey! She did not have a ghost in her Adirondack.

Beulah was greatly disappointed as she rode back home on the almost empty bus in the rain.

Still, she avoided the chair for the next few days.

On Saturday, Laura came over with pecan cookies and fresh lemonade. The weather had cleared and Beulah let her daughter have the Adirondack, while she herself sat in the wicker rocker, hoping they would get a serenade.

Laura sat in the supposedly haunted chair for nearly an hour and there wasn't a peep.

"Mama, why do you insist on having this Yankee piece of furniture?"

"Now, Laura, you know I don't allow that kind of attitude in my house," Beulah said. "I raised you better than that."

"Yes, mama. Still, this chair is mighty uncomfortable, if you ask me, and how the hell do you get yourself up out of it?"

Laura tapped the armrest with her perfectly manicured fingers.

"Really Hon," she continued, "at least let Bobby Joe come by and give this chair a nice quiet makeover with some white or maybe lavender paint."

Yes, Beulah thought. That's what the chair needed all right, a nice *quiet* makeover.

She wondered if the ghost would leave her alone if she had the chair painted pink, like the Cadillac Laura had gotten for selling all that makeup and body lotion. That car was an overstatement of feminine charm, as far as Beulah was concerned.

Maybe the piper would be too much of a man to haunt a pink chair. Then again, the highlander might be a woman, maybe even Millie's naked serenader, who might prefer pink.

No. The chair would stay just as it was. Beulah liked the red just fine and wasn't about to let some old Scottish piper cheat her out of her evening drives in her fiery Maserati.

"No need to bother," Beulah said. "The red perks me up."

Laura had to leave well before sunset to feed her brood of three teenage boys, plus her slow to grow up husband, Bobby Joe.

Beulah would have to face the music alone. She was determined to sit in that chair and stake her claim, *Danny Boy* or no *Danny Boy*, but first she would take a taxi to the Piggly Wiggly and buy herself some bourbon. She never liked to acquire alcohol on her shopping trips with Charmaine. It was not anyone's business what she drank.

Mint julep in hand, Beulah walked with an almost steady, determined gait to the Adirondack just as the sun tucked itself behind the poplars on the western edge of the yard.

She sat in the Adirondack and took a few sips of her drink.

"Come on out now," she coaxed.

Nothing.

"Don't tell me you've gotten shy," she said, a little louder.

Nothing.

"Come out, come out wherever you are!" She shouted.

She was certain the neighbors, should they be out in their yards, would think she was madder than a wet hen, or perhaps they'd only think she had her great grandchildren over for the evening.

The pipes began to croon softly. *If a body meet a body comin' through the rye.*

"Aha!" Beulah whispered, and in a trembling, unsure singing voice answered back, "If a body kiss a body, need a body cry."

The pipes continued with a flourish.

"Oh, you've been practicing your chops, Pops," Beulah said.

The bagpipe switched to something melancholy evoking misted moors and lost love. She didn't recognize it.

"Quite nice," she whispered, relaxing a little. "I'll just have my julep while you play your heart out, and don't worry, I won't be exercising any ghosts this evening. So long as you keep your clothes on and never wake me too early in the morning."

The bagpipes wailed on until all of the pink had drained from the sky and the first stars appeared, bringing cricket song.

Beulah smiled. "Until the morrow," she whispered, standing up and feeling light-headed from the julep, which she had made perhaps a touch too strong.

As she walked towards the house, she noticed something odd over by the forsythia hedge. She strained her eyes to see in the dim light.

"Heavens to Betsy!" she exclaimed.

Standing there, about twenty feet away was the piper himself, in full Scottish regalia, including a red tartan kilt.

Beulah just about fainted, but held her own and walked cautiously a bit closer to the man. He was not altogether there, physically that is, he was a bit hazy, semi-translucent. She could see the forsythia blossoms peeking through his figure as if he were merely a film projected onto the hedge.

Then she saw his face clearly.

"Charlie McGregor?" She exclaimed. "Is that really you?"

She and Charlie had been classmates way back in the fifth-grade. On Valentine's Day that year, he'd given her an entire box of chocolates plus a nervous kiss, right on the lips, right in the middle of the hallway where God and everyone could see it. She'd blushed about the color of the Adirondack. She'd never forgotten it. It was her first kiss.

That summer, Charlie's family moved away to the coast. She never saw him again, until now.

He was older, of course, as old as she was, but he was unmistakably her Charlie.

"My! My! It's good to see you again," Beulah said. "Do play me another song, will you?"

Charlie played one of her favorites, *Georgia*.

Beulah swayed a bit to the tune, feeling as tipsy as she'd felt on that day, so long, long ago.

The Love Tattoo

Time listens like an old crow in the young corn. Hungry. Patient.

Geraldine Maia Jones sits on the porch, her bare feet planted on the boards of the sagging stair like they might never again move from this place of her birth. Her white cotton dress sags between brown knees to ankles swollen from years of travel and high heels. The molecules of wood under her soles resonate with the vibration of the instrument at her chin.

The violin's sensuous form holds steady as rapids of Rachmaninov flow under fluid fingering. She bows the white water tones into the windless sky.

She stops. The weather speaks Gershwin. She turns her face upward into the full flare of sun, her forehead glistening. She adjusts the violin and begins to pull the long, languid notes from the wood. *Summertime.* She nurses the tune. Silver Brown's hound dog howls from its yard down the deserted Sunday morning street. His chewed up ears hear overtones higher than silent stars hiding under cover of heat.

The angels arrive, the old ones who have been here for centuries. They settle on top of the blossom-sown grass, glowing like fireflies in the moist shade. They rest their large, heavy wings with perhaps nothing better to do when good folks are at church and bad folks are sleeping on their couches, wearing yesterday's clothes and last night's liquor on their slow breath.

The angels have come to welcome her.

"We hear you, Sister!" They say.

Gera Maia smiles. She is never alone.

Even as a baby, her mother declared, "That child done talk to the Lord. See them eyes?"

Gera Maia has eyes the color of holy water, opals set in the gentle mahogany of her face. You can't look just once. You have to linger there, even if it is rude, even if you do get uncomfortable with yourself. Those eyes can see straight to your secrets. You can feel it.

She smiles at you, making you flush with the homemade wine of shame. You feel lightheaded when she's laying down a melody because the notes are all the oxygen in the room and you have to breathe them deep or suffocate from the silences between.

It owns her, this music born in the belly of her unanswered soul. She feeds it like a mother cat takes her litter to her teats until she is emptied, sore and red. She is a virtuoso.

That's what the man called her, the tall brother of the Reverend White visiting from Atlanta, wearing a suit the color of elephant tusk and sweating in the humid air from his own excitement. He tells her daddy that Gera Maia is too good to waste on some poor little Baptist church off a dirt road in the dead center of nowhere.

"That child is a virtuoso," he says, his mouth damp at the corners from the weight of the word.

And her daddy lets her go. Her daddy who hardly lets her walk down the road without worrying himself to a sweat, lets his baby girl go to a fancy high school in New York City on a scholarship from the state of Georgia.

That first year, every Friday brings a postcard: Miss Liberty, the Empire State Building, and carriages in Central Park. Her mama carries those cards to all the neighbors' back doors in the lazy hours of the afternoon.

New York is selfish over Gera Maia. She doesn't come home except for summers. She is full of talk then, hard to turn off. So much water pressure she is fixing to burst. So, they let her refresh their minds with that fine, cool spray of talk about city life and music growing into its own knowledge like summer squash so big you wonder how you're going to eat it all and who you can give some to before it spoils.

Everyone at home is like a child then, happy and full of believing in something. Gera Maia's mama cuts a magnolia blossom and floats it on water in her best glass bowl. She lays the food out around it on a faded, blue cloth in the grass, shooing flies off the sweet potato pies.

After New York, comes the University of Chicago. Gera Maia doesn't come home but once a year for Christmas. She says she is too busy.

Her daddy frowns, all of the time fussing with his thoughts, remembering about "nowhere" and how it seems his little girl has come to thinking maybe home isn't good enough for her.

Voices rise during those holiday visits to a place too tight for resolution. Lights stay on late sometimes all night.

Then, there are the concert tours. For almost five years, Gera Maia doesn't come home at all. Every so often, there is a postcard, or a quick, expensive phone call from Los Angeles, Boston, Denver, New York, London, Paris, Moscow.

Eventually, the cards and calls stop coming. There is just a distance without words.

Gera Maia is home today, though.

Her fingers are buzzing with it, with being back at her roots. She turns her spirit-water eyes to the old magnolia of her childhood. It is past blooming. Tattered, cream-colored flowers sulk between oily, green and yellowed leaves.

Gera Maia gets to her feet. Slowly and with effort she moves through the thick silence she has suspended. Her toes dig into the grass. She stands completely in the tree's cooling embrace, branches overhead, and roots below.

She touches its aged bark, looking for the marks she made. Her brother, Kyle, helped her carve them when she was five, holding her hand over the knife.

"Just let me do it, Gera!" He'd whined, kicking his foot into the musty dirt.

"No," she'd said.

That day a fresh petal caressed her cheek.

Now, a wilted petal falls, glides down in the still air and lands on her graying hair.

She feels its gentle weight, takes it in her fingers and lays it against her lips. She leans back against the trunk and eases into memory.

She stands on the polished maple of the stage at Carnegie Hall, the first time.

Her knees are unsure. The orchestra is a tense net of security and expectation behind her. She feels the slick, cool silk of her gown begin to cling to the small of her back, alabaster to ebony.

The music is swollen with anticipation. She feels the taut pull of her imminent entrance. She fills her lungs. The orchestra falls silent.

She drops her full emotional weight down into the bow. Down, into the strident chord. Down, into the electric tension of the strings. High. Suspended. She streaks the silent aural abyss with the call of an eagle, the claim of a warrior.

A thunderclap of timpani and horns lifts her solo onto the arc of a rising canopy of sound, tossing her free into the giddy atmosphere of Beethoven's ethereal mind. Her diamond notes cut the glassy space. She finds her grace over the rugged terrain of musical theory stretched to its extreme edge. She glides with profound focus over the glacial ice of each delicate passage.

She is so young. She is so new. She could easily fall.

She does not fall. An avalanche of applause covers the remnants of her final notes. A crescendo of approval envelops her with the daunting embrace of three-thousand strange hearts.

She stands in triumph. She stands in tears. She stands, listening to the roar of her achievement, wishing her father were here tonight.

She feels the abstract loneliness of fame begin to sip away the nectar of her elation.

In her dressing room, she finds a small, green box with a pale yellow bow. It contains a single magnolia flower, her mother's balm.

An old crow calls from the cornfield behind the house. Time is liquid, fitting any mold. Gera Maia's head rests against the fortitude of her old, patient friend. Her eyes fill with inner rain. She holds the perfumed petal between thumb and middle finger, and returns her forefinger to the tree's weathered skin. She finds the letters there, and runs her finger in the groove of the wood, the old wound, the love tattoo.

A Ride to the Airport

María de la Tierra Sagrada is a dirty town. Not because of pollution, occasional political scandals or a slightly sullied history, but because of the dark red soil that holds its people here.

The holy dirt gets under fingernails, sifts through screened windows in summer and drags through doorways on boot soles in winter.

The town comes out from the sea like beach glass, shiny and opaque, washed and broken again and again, until even its back alleys are beautiful secrets.

The old women here whisper the names of their youthful lovers as if a spell were cast by the very syllables of Jorge, Rafael, Eduardo.

Manuel Alonso walks along the narrow beach, his bare feet within reach of each wave tip that laps at his toes like the tongue of a puppy.

He has been every age on this sand. Skinny Manuelito running toward the ice cream vendor's bell. Shy Mannie, reading novels while studying the boys playing soccer at the surf's edge. Adolescent Manuel, standing under the mango trees with lovely Maria Consuela Alveréz, knowing a kiss was what Maria expected of him, but being able only to stare into her dark eyes. First she looked confused. Then she started to cry.

Manuel's later romantic endeavors did not turn out much better. He remained a bachelor all his life, focused on his work. His passion was pyrography. He burned into leather fantastical birds, lizards, vines and orchids. His work was precise and ornate. It sold well and he eventually owned his own leather shop. His customers said he had inherited his mother's talent.

Manuel's mother painted murals on the walls of his bedroom, thinking that their bright colors and whimsical creatures would distract him from the absence of his father and their poverty. Her elegant peacocks, their tail feathers painted with fine brush strokes, adorned the living room walls. Her jovial blue and red parrots lit up the small kitchen.

His mother stopped painting when she became ill. She died two years later, when Manuel was twenty-one.

He still lives in the little house with her murals, now faded to pastels. He keeps her paintbrushes wrapped in a cloth at the back of a dresser drawer. Her tubes of oil paint dried up long ago.

Under the bridge, where the river moves into the sea like a question mark, Manuel almost drowned at twenty-two.

On that morning, during the hurricane named Alma, he was swept away by an angry wave.

He had wanted to be swept away, but then he'd held his breath longer than the patience of Death, despite drowning in sorrow.

Death took many lives that day but spared the inhabitants of María de la Tierra Sagrada, though a furious wind sent mangoes flying through the streets like bullets, hitting walls with yellow fury and smacking old Paco Gomez so hard in the forehead, he passed out. A lucky thing for him, as he fell just in time to miss decapitation by the tin roof of his outhouse slicing through the air.

Manuel stares at the calm sea. Today, he is leaving them all behind. He is not leaving because he has grown tired of this small paradise in need of paint and maintenance, or because he no longer loves these dusty houses with their cacti-infested courtyards and sweltering bedchambers.

He is leaving because a heart broken as many times as his own is a dark omen for the younger and untried. He is leaving because those who have broken his heart are all gone and there is no longer any reason to forgive.

He will wait for the público at the north end of town. It will take him to the airport. He has told no one of his plan. They would think him crazy, but he is only an old man with a dream to see his mother's country and let his tired bones rest there when he is gone. Death has been patient with him all these years but Manuel's own patience has run dry.

He sits for a moment on the crumbling wall above the beach. The sea is peaceful. He places his old fedora on the wall beside him and leans down to brush the sand from his feet. He slips on his worn leather sandals with the peacock feather pattern on the straps. He replaces his hat and walks slowly up the hill to wait in the shade of the mango trees.

He stands there alone at first, then a few others arrive. The butcher, Victor Itxaro and his wife, Alma. The teenaged Ignazio brothers, who lean against the tree trunks wearing cheap dark sunglasses.

Hadria Fortuna, skinny and stubborn as a dried reed, who wobbles down the hill with her basket of woven cloth for market. Some say she is a witch because of the strong smell of bitter herbs that emanates from her old clothes and her wild white hair.

The público comes down from the mountains. Its boxy pink shape moves along the switchbacks and the clatter of its diesel engine grows louder at each turn. The bus is late by nearly an hour. Manuel is not concerned. The flight he has booked will not be leaving until late afternoon. He plans to eat a simple meal at the airport's cafeteria while waiting.

The público comes to a stop with a screech of brakes, a cloud of dust and a black plume of exhaust. Its rusty doors groan open. Once the leaving passengers step off, those waiting ascend the rickety metal stairs. Manuel drops his coins into the slot of the fare box. Each one clangs like a bell.

The Ignazio brothers plop into their seats. Hadria Fortuna shuffles down the aisle ahead of Manuel. She stops towards the back of the bus.

"You take the window," she commands Manuel. "I do not like to see the world go by so fast."

They settle into their seats. A feisty cumbia sputters through static from the small radio strapped to the front windshield beneath the rearview mirror. All the window mechanisms are broken and the windows are stuck open at various heights.

Manuel sits in the seat over the rear left tire and every pothole sends him up off the cushion for a moment before settling back down with a squeak from the springs. He wants to move to another seat but that requires asking Hadria Fortuna to get up. Not a pleasant prospect. Despite the relentless bouncing, Hadria has already fallen asleep, her head resting on the basket of rainbow woven cloth in her lap. She snores loudly and smells of talcum, sage, and the passing of years.

As the bus ascends into the mountains, there is a light morning mist. It feels refreshingly cool coming in through the opened windows and Manuel is grateful for it.

At every stop, the driver lets on a few more people. Two wrinkled campesinos. A shy girl with a black kitten, accompanied by her extraordinarily lovely mother. Two nuns in their black habits. Four schoolgirls in the plaid uniforms of San Ignacio. Soon the small bus rides heavy on its worn shocks.

The airport lies in a wide valley on the other side of the mountains. The terminal is dingy with grimy windows. It hums with flies, smelling of fried onions and aftershave. In the waiting areas, the worn vinyl seats are repaired with duct tape over many tears in the cushions.

Manuel has never taken a flight but the bus into the city departs from the airport terminal. He used to take that bus once a month to sell his handmade leather goods at the outdoor market. He has not gone in many years now. It is too difficult for his old hands to do the leather sewing. He sold his shop and lives on a government pension.

Manuel pulls out a book, but it is impossible to keep a steady hand, the road is a washboard. The words jump around on the page and he is unable to connect them for meaning. He gives up and tucks his glasses back into his pocket. He closes his eyes and smells the wetness of leaves and the aroma of rotting guavas as he feels himself drift over the threshold between wakefulness and sleep.

The público turns abruptly to the left. Manuel jostles fully awake. If his memory serves him, the driver should have continued straight on the main road.

Perhaps the driver knows a shorter route, or perhaps they will become lost.

It doesn't matter to Manuel. There are still many hours before he is at risk of missing his flight. Besides, he is far too old to argue with the driver, who has a bulldog tattoo on his bulging bicep.

Manuel gazes out of his open window. The foliage along the road is thick, lithe branches occasionally flick inside. He pulls the brim of his fedora over his eyes. The air is rich with the calls of tree frogs and birds as the público churns upwards. The road's many tight turns are making him a bit queasy. He places his hat on his lap and wipes the sweat from his forehead with his sleeve.

Up in the mountains the vegetation is a tropical jungle. Bromeliads grow on the escarpment of reddish mud. The driver is singing loudly with the radio and swerving dangerously back and forth along the narrow road, not always staying on the correct side.

Manuel feels slightly faint. He turns to talk with Hadria Fortuna, but she has become a mangy goat and her bearded chin is shaking as she laughs.

"Look at you, Manuelito!" she says. "So much you have lost and so little to show for it. So little!"

Hadria bites into the cloth in her basket and chews with great satisfaction as Manuel stares at the hair around her watery, pink eyes. She appears huge, towering above him.

Manuel feels ashamed and looks at his feet. They are tiny. The tiny feet of a mouse.

"¡Madre de Dios!" he gasps.

Manuel scrambles to the top of his seat back and digs his sharp little mouse claws into the upholstery. From there he can see everything.

The bus sputters, threatening to stop, then lurches forward, sending the Ignazio brothers flying from their seats.

As they cry out, their tanned, muscular bodies change into long-armed monkeys. They grab onto the baggage racks and swing over the heads of passengers.

There is general mayhem until the driver's voice crackles over the loudspeaker.

"¡Amigos y amigas! Por favor, cálmese."

The monkeys settle down up front and begin grooming each other.

The old goat is now standing in the aisle, nibbling on the stuffing that protrudes from a seat cushion.

Manuel no longer recognizes the road. The tires must be hugging the edge of a sheer cliff. From his perch, he can see across the aisle and out of the windows on the opposite side. The view is dizzying.

He squeaks. The minuscule sound of his own voice frightens him.

The giggling schoolgirls turn into red and blue parrots. They squawk and fly out of a window, up into the foliage.

The bus is driving so close to the mud escarpment now that Manuel can smell the bromeliads and ferns, the raw fecundity of the moist soil. He wants to jump from the bus but is too afraid.

Two campesinos a few rows ahead, shed their human forms to become silver snakes. They slither over their seat backs.

Manuel's small mouse belly tightens. He is relieved when the snakes slip out of the window and up into the ferns.

The driver smiles into the rearview mirror instead of watching the road as he transforms into a massive iguana.

"Please fasten your seat belts," he hisses.

There are no seatbelts and even if there were, what use would they be to a mouse?

As the bus careens along the precipice, he hangs on to the upholstery and prays to the Virgin, or anyone who might be listening.

He can hear the transmission shift down to a lower gear. The road ahead disappears. The monkeys shout with glee as the bus pulls out into the blue sky, the front and rear tires spinning free in the air.

Through the side window, Manuel sees the vast expanse of the valley thousands of feet below and the runways of the airport in the distance, like charcoal pencil marks on a field of pale green.

The two nuns in the front row turn into white doves. They fly through an open window with a flutter of feathers and a light chink as their rosary beads hit the metal window frame.

As the front of the bus tips downward, the goat slides on her furry butt in the aisle. Manuel falls from his perch and lands in Hadria's basket of cloth. He burrows down into the soft darkness.

Then, he hears a loud snap, like the sound of cloth in the wind. The bus swings in the opposite direction. Hadria's basket is sent flying. Manuel squeals like a frightened child on an amusement park ride.

He peeks out from the basket and sees the goat sliding the other way down the aisle past him. Just as everything in the baggage compartments begins to fall out, Hadria's basket slides under a seat where Manuel is protected from being crushed. He burrows back into the folds.

There is no sound except a low creaking, like the timbers of an old boat at sea. The bus sways from side to side.

Manuel's stomach feels green and his mouth tastes sour, but he is too curious to stay hidden. He crawls out of the basket, scampers over the sticky floor and climbs back up to the top of a seat back.

The bus is drifting in the direction of the airport.

Manuel jumps onto the narrow window sill and looks up. A huge white parachute has opened above. It is beautiful.

He weeps softly. They are mouse tears but they are his tears.

"Querido Dios," he whispers. "Por favor, don't let me die a mouse."

His tiny body shivers. His whiskers brush against the glass pane, sending a creepy tingling through his face.

He closes his eyes.

"I just want to be Manuelito again. I was so small my whole life. Let me make it up to you."

He waits, keeping his eyes closed.

When he opens them again, he looks up into the white arch of the parachute. It glows in the sunlight.

The iguana's shrill voice interrupts his reverie.

"Damas y caballeros, prepare for landing!"

The iguana guides the bus into position over a runway in a steep descent.

Manuel falls down into the seat cushion below and holds onto the upholstery with all his might.

The ground reaches up to grab the bus which bounces violently several times before coming to an abrupt halt.

There is a moment of quiet, a hush.

Then, the entire bus erupts into cheers.

Manuel's high-pitched squeal ends as a low guttural sigh of relief.

He glances down and sees his shoes, with his feet inside. His old man's feet. He touches his face. No more whiskers, just his own small mustache.

"Gracias," he says softly.

The doors of the bus open with a moan demanding oil. The driver is back in his burly human body and sweat-stained shirt. The remaining passengers, those who did not leap, fly or crawl from the bus as animals, are all back in their human forms. They gather their belongings and head towards the front of the bus.

Manuel thinks about the two campesinos who became snakes. Those old men are probably lying among the ferns, their mouths full of dirt. He hopes the two nuns who became doves were allowed to fly all the way to heaven. Why not, after all?

The shy girl with the black kitten wears a radiant smile. Her mother has tears running down her cheeks. Manuel offers her crying mother the clean white handkerchief from his breast pocket. She accepts it with a nod.

The Ignazio brothers are up to their fidgety antics. The goat is once again Hadria Fortuna. Even for her, Manuel feels some fondness as she shuffles to the front mumbling.

He watches the motley crew walk over the tarmac towards the terminal. They will be taking the bus into the city.

He reaches for his leather bag in the luggage bin. It is not there. He looks around and eventually finds it under the rear bench seat. He retrieves it and moves slowly to the front of the bus.

The driver smiles, his gruff exterior momentarily forgotten, his iguana skin a distant memory.

"Déjame ayudarte, viejo," the driver says, getting out of his seat, and he cradles Manuel's arm as they descend the rickety stairs.

Manuel walks across the hot tarmac and enters the terminal. It is cool inside.

He hardly recognizes the place. There are new seats in the waiting areas with shiny chrome frames and intact black vinyl. Soft music is wafting from somewhere in the ceiling. He detects a slight scent of gardenias.

He sits down to regain some composure. The new seats are comfortable. When was the last time he smiled. He smiles.

His elderly neighbor, Maria Fuentes, will need help harvesting her garden now that her grandson has moved to the city. Wild parrots come each morning to eat the sunflower seeds he leaves on the windowsill. They are always so happy to have those seeds.

He thinks about what the goat said, that he has so little to show for his life.

When he gets back home, Manuel decides, he will take his mother's brushes from the dresser, buy some fresh oil paints and canvas and try his hand at painting.

His airline ticket is just a jumble of numbered codes, times of departure and arrival at a destination that now seems impossibly far away.

He grabs his bag and walks with determination towards the check-in area.

There is no line, so he steps up to the counter.

"May I help you, señor?" a young woman with a short haircut asks.

Manuel looks into her serious eyes.

"Death will have to wait," he says.

The ticket agent looks at him as if she's not sure he is in his right mind.

Manuel hands her his ticket. "You see, I have decided not to go. Is it possible to receive a refund?"

The agent scrutinizes the ticket. "No, señor, but you can use the airfare toward a new ticket for up to two years. Do you wish to cancel your flight today?"

"Sí, por favor."

The agent punches information into her computer. She writes something on the ticket and returns it to him.

"Bring this to any travel agency or back here when you are ready to reschedule."

Manuel takes the cancelled ticket from her hand and places it back inside his bag.

He walks toward the airport's cafeteria, feeling like a much younger man, and suddenly hungry.

The cafeteria has been replaced by a proper restaurant with tables and stately wooden chairs. He has the money for the suit he'd planned to wear. He no longer needs the suit.

He sits at a small table by a tall window and reads the fancy menu. He orders a steak grilled with green peppers, some seasoned rice with avocado slices and a shot glass of expensive tequila.

The tequila arrives first.

Manuel raises his glass into the air.

"¡Salud!" he says with glee, to no one in particular.

Happy travels!

With Gratitude

Many thanks to Elisabeth Appels,
Patrick Markham and Alethea Eason
for all of their brilliant support.

About the Author

Eve West Bessier is an award-winning author of fiction, essays and poetry. She was born in the Netherlands and immigrated to the United States with her mom at age seven. Eve is a poet laureate emerita of Silver City, New Mexico and of Davis, California. She worked as a social scientist, educator and voice coach. Eve loves singing jazz, playing the drums, hiking and taking photographs in nature. You can find out more and watch performance videos on her website.

www.jazzpoeteve.com

Made in the USA
Middletown, DE
31 August 2022

72766103R00087